Abandon

The "A" Word Romances, Volume 1

Jerusha Moors

Published by Sunday Morning Publishing, 2015.

ABANDON

First edition. August 2, 2015.

ISBN: 979-8201214074

Written by Jerusha Moors.

Chapter One

"Lovell, man, please tell me we can leave this tedious ball and find better amusement elsewhere." Edward Pryce, Earl of Thornton, was a handsome man and never more so when he dressed in formal black evening attire. But he was in profound fear of the white-clad debutantes and their eagle-eyed mamas who stood observing the small group of men clustered near the terrace doors. Thornton edged around the group, keeping his back to the wall, his height giving him an advantage in observing any women encroaching too close to them.

Aubrey St Clare, Viscount Lovell, grimaced. "I promised both my dear mama and our good friend George I would stay for the supper dance. Once that occurs, we can leave with all due haste and go to the club for something better to drink than what we have here."

Thornton rolled his eyes. "Surely we can find a better place than White's to spend the rest of our night. Perhaps that new gaming hell with a visit to the brothel next door would shake you out of your doldrums."

"Lovell is too much of a saint now to even think of such entertainments. He left those diversions behind at school, or perhaps in Italy." Harry Wilton, Lord Blakesley, affected a drawl. "Although I don't understand why you care what your mother says when you have no intention of marrying soon. You have only just returned from your years abroad. I'm sure she can give you some leeway and time to find a bride."

Aubrey shrugged. "I am here for George since he's the first of our little company to get leg-shackled. He and Lady Harriet asked we attend as it is their engagement ball. But I did not agree to dance or even converse with any of the young ladies present." He gazed around the brightly lit ballroom, his eyes hard and expression stern.

Blakesley laughed. "I swear those two young ladies standing with Lady Austen took two steps backward when you glared at them just now. You have most assuredly dashed any hopes they might have had by your attendance tonight."

Thornton smirked. "Perhaps they have designs on you and your estate, Blakesley, old man, instead of Lovell. Your time is drawing near as well."

"I don't fear that, Thornton, with you in the room. All the mamas here are estimating your income, and the young ladies are in worship of your godlike Greek looks." Blakesley was a good-looking man but knew his appearance would always come in second to any of his friends. Thornton did, in truth, look like Apollo with his blond hair curling over his collar and his blue eyes creased with laugh lines in his striking face. He loved to ride and fence, and his body exhibited a powerful form that attracted notice, his shoulders broad under the fine linen of his coat.

"I believe Lovell will win any contest with the ladies. His Byronic looks and mysterious travels attract the attention of all, and his disdain for the fairer sex only ensures their notice. Nothing is more guaranteed to draw notice from the ladies than indifference. And he is new 'meat,' so to speak." Thornton didn't appear worried about competition.

Aubrey snorted in an inelegant manner. "I am no one's 'meat' I'll have you know. And I do not intend to marry — ever. My cousin can have the title and estates with my thanks, no matter what my mother may say."

"I think Lady Harriet will have something to say about it. She's been casting a gimlet eye on us all since the dancing began. Now she has caught Aversley in her coils, she will be matchmaking for his friends, I fear." Blakesley didn't appear too concerned, but Thornton lifted his head and examined the room with care as if afraid Lady Harriet Everton had him in her sights and was dragging a young ingenue over for him to wed.

"Relax, Thornton. Lady Harriet is much too busy tonight to bother with finding your future bride." Aubrey sighed and then straightened as a young woman in a pale pink dress clasped her hands together to her breast and gazed at him with appreciation. He rolled his eyes and turned his back with care, not wanting to give the young miss any encouragement.

Blakesley had seen the entire incident and barked a laugh. "I think Thornton has the right of it. The less assurance you give to the ladies, the more they believe they can be the one to catch their elusive prey."

Aubrey grimaced. It would be a long few weeks until George, Baron Aversley, celebrated his nuptials to Lady Harriet. Until that time, Aubrey, Blakesley, and Thornton were under strict orders to attend the many fetes and luncheons leading up to the grand event. Thornton and Blakesley would do their duty with minimal effort, escaping to the card rooms or their clubs when allowed. Aubrey, who was closest to Aversley and who would stand up with him at the wedding, needed to maintain a more public appearance. It didn't matter he had just returned to England after five years abroad and had many duties towards his estates to fulfill. His father had been ill for several months leading to his death last year. The manager left in charge hadn't maintained it as he should or, at least, Aubrey needed to determine if that was true. It'd taken time for word to reach him in La Spezia of his father's demise, and even then he had delayed his return. He could no longer put it off when the letter from George had arrived announcing his upcoming nuptials and asking for Aubrey's support.

"Smile, Lovell, smile. That sad face will never win fair maiden," Thornton joined in the banter. His grin faded as another matron glided too close to the three men for his comfort. "Perhaps we should adjourn to the card room for the nonce."

"Ah, Carlisle has arrived. And he has Lady Lucilla on his arm. I hadn't realized she came down from the North," Blakesley said with a sneer. "I can't believe he brought her here."

"What do you mean? She is Lady Harriet's attendant. Of course, she would attend the engagement ball." Thornton disapproved of Blakesley's tendency to gossip.

Aubrey felt an icy tendril chase down his back. He casually asked, "Lady Lucilla?" He would not turn to the door to look, he could not move, his feet frozen in place. But the prickling on the back of his neck let him know who arrived even before Blakesley spoke.

Blakesley replied, unperturbed by Thornton's frown, "Lady Lucilla Blount, the Earl of Wakefield's sister. You remember Richard Blount. He was ahead of us by a few years at Oxford. He married a girl from York or Shropshire, Anne someone or other, a few years ago."

Thornton sniffed. "Lady Lucilla is quite respectable now. The Duke of Carlisle is great friends with Wakefield, and he has rehabilitated her reputation. I heard a rumor he intends to marry her and make her his Duchess, so she will outrank you in the end. I wouldn't sneer at Carlisle's intended if I were you."

Aubrey was sweating now and had gone pale under the tan he still wore from the hot Italian sun. This was his worst nightmare, Lucilla here and not married or betrothed. He had never asked, but he thought for a surety she must have had a triumphant Season and married almost at once after it. The men in London *must* have recognized her unique manner and outstanding beauty when she had her come out. He hadn't seen her in over five years, but the memories he carried far transcended the reality of any other woman present in the room.

Thornton and Blakesley were still squabbling over Carlisle and his companion. Aubrey tried to compose himself since his two distracted friends didn't notice his agitation. He took a deep breath and turned casually toward the entrance to the ballroom. A tall ginger-headed man stood there speaking to George and Lady Harriet. He was tall and good-looking with the aristocratic bearing of his ducal forbears.

Aubrey could see no one with him. Where was she? And then George stepped back, revealing the subject of his dreams and of his despairing nightmares.

Lucy had changed. She was still slender, but no longer a girl. She had blossomed into a stunning and elegant woman. Her chestnut hair was in some loose arrangement, not curling over her shoulders like the last time he'd seen her. She wore a pale peach gown, low-cut in a manner that displayed much more cleavage than he remembered and by god, he still remembered every inch of her body. He wanted to rip the shawl off of the Dowager Countess of Hereford and rush over to cover that pale display. She was too far away for him to see her eyes, but it didn't matter. He'd never forget them. Those chocolate brown eyes dominated her heart-shaped face and were the gateway to her soul. She couldn't hide what she thought when you looked in her eyes.

Aubrey's breath seized in his chest, and he thought he might faint. This was so much worse than he had ever dreamed, and he had envisioned their meeting many times. He tugged on his cravat and spun on his heel, "I need some air" as he walked towards the terrace doors, trying not to run in his panic.

Once he was outside, he rushed off the terrace, down the stairs to the garden. There was a bench below, the terrace railing above it and he sank down, head in his hands and mind in a whirl. Aubrey drew in a deep gasp of air, trying to regulate his breathing and regain his composure. He closed his eyes and leaned his head back against the wall behind him. He would take a moment and then try to consider how he would slip away.

Chapter Two

Lady Lucilla Blount gave every appearance of icy reserve. She wouldn't let Carlisle down. He was her dear friend and did not deserve disapprobation from his peers on her account. She knew she was in good looks tonight, a fit companion for a Duke, even if her decolletage might be a trifle low for a single woman. But she was no longer a girl, and most considered her on the shelf so she would do as she pleased as long as Harriet and Carlisle weren't adverse.

In truth, she was nervous. She hated Ton affairs and seldom came to town after the spectacular failure of her first Season. She couldn't abide the gossip that still ran rampant about her. But Harriet wanted her here to celebrate her wedding to George, Baron Aversley. Dearest George, he treated Harriet so well, and she deserved all the best. Lucy smiled at her friend where she stood on George's arm, triumphant in her happiness. George's mother, a witch in Lucy's opinion, thought her son could do much better, even if George were in love with Harriet, the youngest daughter of the dissolute Earl of Brandwine. But Harriet was sweet and pretty, just as in love with George as he was her. Though loth to cause a rift with his mother, George dug his heels in, and his mother was currently rusticating at his country home, on probation until she could behave herself at the pre-wedding festivities.

Carlisle looked down at her and patted her hand where it rested on his arm, reassuring her he was here to support her, even if no one else spoke to her this evening. As if anyone here would gainsay the Duke of Carlisle or disparage her in front of him. It would be the subtle cuts in the ladies retiring room or pointed remarks spoke just as she passed the ladies of the ton would use to show their contempt for her. Even worse would be the leering glances of the men and the rubbing too close, the too-tight embraces if she danced. Surely she had paid enough penance for the wildness of a grieving girl, allowed too much freedom in her first bid at society.

"Lucy, please smile. Reassure me I did the right thing in dragging you from your Northern stronghold." Harriet clasped Lucilla close and whispered in her ear. Harriet drew back and examined her friend, seeing the tautness of her lips and the worry in her eyes. "I *need* you here, and I want you to share my happiness." Harriet chewed at her lower lip, a nervous habit that just endeared her all the more to Lucy.

She pushed a stray curl behind Harriet's ear and gave a little smile. "Oh, my dear, you know I am most happy for you. George is mad for you and will do all possible to make you an excellent life. I am so envious."

"He is perfect, is he not?" Harriet beamed. "But, Lucy," she whispered, "what about Carlisle? Could you not find the same happiness with him?"

Lucy tensed, but she answered all the same. "Carlisle is my dear friend and nothing more. I don't expect ever to find the ideal man such as you have discovered in George and I am resigned to my fate." Lucy grinned. "But dear, you and George must circulate amongst your guests. Do not worry, Carlisle will take good care of me."

Harriet nodded and looked up at George by her side, her eyes shining. His look was just as tender as he drew her away to speak to the Countess of Lisle and her three marriageable daughters. They were all glaring daggers at Lucy while trying to simper at Carlisle at the same time. She sighed again, and Carlisle looked down. He was so tall even if she wasn't petite.

"Would you like to dance?" he asked. "Or perhaps you'd prefer a refreshment?"

Lucilla gazed around the crowded ballroom. No one was giving her the cut, but neither did anyone look friendly. Several of the rakes who would be all too welcoming if she went anywhere near them without Carlisle at her side were the only exceptions.

"Perhaps some air would be invigorating. It seems so warm in here, don't you think?"

Carlisle murmured in agreement and guided her to the terrace doors on the far side of the room. He received greetings and acknowledgments as they passed though none were for her. But he held her arm and kept by her side, dispensing icy stares at any of the dowagers who were too pointed in their disapproval.

No one was on the terrace, and Lucy finally relaxed. She walked to the railing, staring out at the dark gardens. Carlisle stopped a few steps back, and she could feel him staring at her back. Lucy closed her eyes and tensed. In her haste to remove herself from the glares in the ballroom, Lucy had placed herself in a more awkward situation. She'd known this moment was coming; it was one reason she delayed her arrival in London until today. But she did not want to have this conversation now — or at all.

"Lucilla." His voice was low and seductive in the dark.

"Jamie, please." Lucy turned to look over her shoulder, hoping to put him off for at least one more day, just until she felt a little stronger. She didn't want to hurt him, but she needed more time to find the right words to make that happen. She could tell he wanted no more delays, and Lucy bowed her head, awaiting the inevitable.

"Lucilla, you know I have the utmost regard and affection for you." Carlisle had taken her fingers into one of his big hands while he tipped her face up with the other, so she had to look into his earnest, dear face. "I am sure your brother would approve, and I would do all in my power to make you happy. Would you do I the honor of accepting my declaration of respect and admiration for you and make me the happiest man on earth?"

A sound from the garden below distracted Lucy. Was someone down there? But Jamie had not moved, was still staring at her, his question unanswered, and she needed to settle this. She reached up and placed her gloved hand at the side of his face.

"Jamie, you do me the greatest of honors." She spoke with precision, determined to find the exact words that would somehow keep Jamie as a friend. James Lennox, Duke of Carlisle, was a handsome, wealthy man who would make any woman a wonderful husband. But he deserved a woman whom he could love and who would love him in return. He was too good a friend, and Lucy would not take his generous sacrifice, even if he were willing.

"It is no good, my dear. You will not have me?"

She had taken too much time, and Jamie had drawn the proper conclusion. He was always too astute in reading Lucy. He'd been her friend since her first Season when he stood by her in the muddle she'd made.

"I cannot. I love you so much as a friend and brother. But I will never marry. You should find a more suitable companion, a lady to marry and love you how you deserve." Lucy's heart ached, her entire body tense as she hoped Jamie would understand. He lifted his free hand to cover the small hand she still held to the side of his face.

"You know I find you suitable or I would not have asked." Carlisle was gentle but firm.

"Yes, I know, and I much appreciate your friendship and how you've supported me in these last years. Richard is also grateful for your aid in rehabilitating our name which I so disgraced in the eyes of the Ton." The bitterness with which she said this surprised Lucy. She thought she'd recovered from that mad first Season by now. Her current life was pleasurable and serene which was what she wanted.

So she tried for a lighter tone. "I intend to live my life at home with only occasional trips to town. It is relaxing there. I would be there now if not for Harriet. It isn't the life the Duchess of Carlisle must lead. She must be a leader of the Ton, holding balls and gracing social affairs. I could not make you happy." She leaned her forehead against his broad chest. If anyone came out on the terrace and saw her, she'd be compromised once more, but she wanted to give him some comfort if she could, and she would deal with any fallout later.

Carlisle stepped back, though, correct as always. He did not smile, but Lucy thought his face, while not smiling, had relaxed, and the tightness around his eyes had eased.

"I wish you felt otherwise, my dear. You are too young to give up all hope of husband and family. Do you not want children of your own someday?" His kind face tempted her, and Lucy thought her heart might break, but she couldn't give in. It would be a good life with Jamie, placid and unruffled, and her ducal status would force the Ton to accept her, if reluctantly. But she had a life of her own she would not leave, and he had his own duties and responsibilities. There would never be the passion she once had. For a moment, the idea tempted her, but she could not do it.

Slowly Lucilla shook her head, and Carlisle seemed finally to concede. "Then I suppose we should return to the ballroom. Perhaps you might grace me with a dance?"

Lucilla stared into his face in the light of the torches on the terrace, but his eyes crinkled, and he gave her a small smile that reassured there was no heartbreak on either side, maybe just a little regret. And she knew how to live with disappointment. She took his arm and turned back to the doors.

Below in the gardens, Aubrey St. Clare stared into the darkness beyond him, stunned by what he overheard. Lucy should have accepted the man's offer, he thought. And it was his fault.

Chapter Three

Aubrey St. Clare, Viscount Lovell, wasn't in a hurry as he strolled down Bond Street. He had an appointment with his bootmaker, and after ordering his boots, he had a few more errands before he stopped at his club. Aubrey intended to visit Lackington Allen's to find new books for his library. It was a sunny day, and shoppers crowded the streets, browsing the windows and covertly observing other members of the Ton. Aubrey ignored them all, being much too caught up in his own thoughts to pay them any mind. They were not happy thoughts so the scowl on his face was enough to warn off any who might have thought to interrupt his deliberations. Two young ladies who might have tried to catch his attention turned to each other as they passed him. A display of ribbons seemed much safer to inspect than the moody Viscount.

His mind was in a whirl, and that was not a state Aubrey liked. He'd grown accustomed to the serenity of Italy, the brilliant sunshine on the dark green olive trees, the blue of the Mediterranean Sea. Aubrey lived in solitary comfort there, just his housekeeper to tend him and cook simple meals. He was an ordinary man to the people in the village, an artist and mad Englishman, who lived a quiet life.

His father's death forced him back to England. There was business to take care of, the affairs of his estate, and he needed to look after his mother. Responsibility did not bother him; his father had trained Aubrey for it, and he accepted the necessity for this duty, but Lucy's appearance at the ball last night had knocked him off his pins. He'd not gotten a wink of sleep, consuming too much of the brandy in his library. He kept going over and over in his head the conversation he had overheard on the terrace between Lucy and Carlisle. Then he had ruined a perfectly good canvas, unable to concentrate on the scene he wanted, seeing only Lucy in his mind's eye, lush and pale in the candlelight.

Why *wasn't* she married? Bloody hell, what was the matter with Wakefield? Shouldn't he have found her a husband by now? He stopped in the middle of the sidewalk, regardless of the people passing by him, and closed his eyes as he remembered her appearance at the ball. She was still as beautiful as ever. He groaned and shook his head, then realized where he was and walked again, ignoring the stares and whispers behind hands.

A bell chimed as a millinery shop door opened to let a few women exit the store. Too late Aubrey recognized Lady Harriet, followed by Lucy and a maid carrying wrapped parcels.

"Lord Lovell," Harriet exclaimed. "How nice to meet you again and so soon. I do hope you enjoyed yourself last evening."

Aubrey nodded his head, not daring to risk a glance at Lucy. "It was quite enjoyable, Lady Harriet. I trust you and Aversley also had a pleasurable evening. The ballroom was sparkling, and it was such a crush." Aubrey realized he was blathering on and took a deep breath, forcing himself to stop. He turned to her companion.

Lucilla was not even looking at him but was staring fixedly at something further down the street. She gave nothing away, no knowledge she even knew him but stood still as a statue. She was beautiful in a yellow walking dress, a bonnet tipped with a long green feather trailing off the back, set just so on her thick chestnut hair. Only the small hands fisted within her gloves exposed her tension.

"I trust you have met Lady Lucilla Blount," Harriet was introducing them. "Lucilla, Viscount Lovell is a dear friend of Aversley and will stand for him at our wedding."

A flash of memory went through Aubrey's mind, long pale limbs and chestnut hair tumbling over rounded pink-tipped breasts. Oh, yes, he knew her. Sweat was dripping down his back, and he could feel the flush on the back of his neck.

"It has been quite a long time, but—" he got no further. Lucy looked at him square in the eyes, lifted her arm, and slapped him hard across the face. Then she pushed past him and strode down the street.

Lady Harriet's eyes were wide and her face flushed. "Oh, dear," she exclaimed. "I don't, I mean, I'm not sure..." her voice trailed off helplessly.

Aubrey straightened his shoulders and forced a smile. "I'm sure she mistook me for someone else. There is a misunderstanding of some sort, I'm sure." The maid dropped a package, distracting Lady Harriet, and Aubrey bent to aid her and recover himself at the same time.

He handed her the parcel, something soft wrapped in brown paper, and bowed. "I'm sure you have more errands, so I'll let you be on your way." He knew he sounded stilted, but he needed to get away himself. The altercation had attracted the attention of the other shoppers, and he could sense curious looks.

"Of course, I must catch up with Lady Lucilla." The incident had flustered poor Harriet. "I hope to meet you again soon. I'm sure our paths will cross." She curtsied and hurried off down the street, followed by her maid. Aubrey turned and could just see the feather in Lucilla's bonnet where she waited for the others some ways further down the street. He sighed and turned away.

By the time Aubrey reached his club, he was more than ready for a brandy. His mind was spinning, going over and over the incident on the street. Lord, she must hate him if she would make such a scene in public. Aubrey deserved it even if his heart hurt at the thought. He absently rubbed his chest, trying to ease the ache as he looked around the room.

Aubrey spied Blakesley sitting in a comfortable chair in a corner and sat down next to him, signaling for a drink. He tipped his head back while he waited for the waiter and sighed, looking around the room. A lot of the men seemed to send sly looks his way which meant that talk about him and Lucy was already about.

Blakesley looked over, a smirk on his face. "I heard you had an interesting confrontation today."

Aubrey sighed again, sure that Blakesley was too much of a gossip to let this go.

"I believe Lady Lucilla mistook me for another gentleman. Remember that I have been out of the country the last several years."

"But isn't her brother's estate in Yorkshire near your own lands?" No, Blakesley would not let the incident go.

The waiter served Aubrey's drink, and he took a moment to swallow, letting the rich liquor burn its way to his stomach and clear his head.

"Well, yes, but it's been many years since I've seen her. We were just children, and she was an acquaintance of my family and much younger than me." Aubrey disliked dishonesty but thought the circumstances justified some prevarication.

Aversley and Thornton's arrival interrupted them; they'd been at Tattersalls looking at a pair of matched chestnuts for Thornton's new brougham.

"So, Lovell, what is this I hear of fisticuffs with Lady Lucilla?" It did not appear that his encounter with Lucilla was passé yet. Thornton looked amused, but Aversley was not happy.

"What was all that about? Lady Harriet is most upset. And that makes me even more distressed! We can't have the members of the marriage party in open disagreement with each other."

Aubrey tried to soothe Aversley's ruffled feathers. He was a good fellow, and the stress of his upcoming nuptials along with his mother's disapproval made him sensitive to his betrothed's feelings in Aubrey's opinion. But what did he know?

"I was just explaining it to Blakesley. The girl's family lives next to my estate in Yorkshire. She was younger than me, and I suppose she might have a childish grudge or perhaps mistook me for someone else." Aubrey felt the back of his neck getting hot. This was getting worse and worse.

Blakesley interrupted, "The girl is bad blood, anyway. Her first season was a disgrace, and she has got no better as the years have gone by."

Aubrey lifted his head, staring at Blakesley. Aversley's face turned a dull red, and his eyes narrowed. "What the blazes are you talking about? Lady Lucilla Blount is an elegant lady, sister to the Earl of Wakefield, and excellent Ton. She is Harriet's best friend, and I won't have you speak ill of her."

"All right, George. Calm down. I do not intend that you call me out over this," Blakesley replied his hands out and palms up in a conciliatory manner. "But you have to admit that her birth was irregular, don't you? After all, she admitted it herself."

Aubrey paled and sank back into his chair. How did they know? And how had Lucy discovered the truth? He reached for his brandy and took a deep gulp, the liquid burning down his throat, causing him to break out into a fit of coughing. Blakesley and Aversley broke off their disagreement to stare at him with concern.

Thornton reached over and patted Aubrey on the back. One eyebrow lifted in a manner that conveyed he did not believe the choking fit was an accident. His next words confirmed the sentiment.

"Do you have a problem with Lady Lucilla's birth lines?" He inquired. "For if her father and his wife did not, I do not see why society should care. It's not like she's the heir. And the actual heir considers her his sister which she is as they share the same father. Richard was friends with my brother, Edmund, and confided as much during Lady Lucilla's first season. Edmund had an interest in her, but then the scandal made her ineligible for him. And then he died." Face blank, Thornton sat back, crossed his legs, and tugged at a sleeve, looking for all the world like a judge who had just delivered a critical verdict.

Blakesley sniffed, thwarted in his opinion while Aversley openly gloated. Thornton had been the arbitrator of their little band since Oxford days, and his opinion ruled.

"Father?" Aubrey clung to the one word that made the most amount of sense to him in a discussion that seemed utterly incomprehensible.

Blakesley cast a snide look at Aversley. He replied, "Lady Lucilla's father is the deceased Earl of Wakefield, but her mother was not the former Lady Wakefield, just the Earl's mistress, a plump widow he kept stashed away nearby."

"No, that's not right," Aubrey said, confused. "Lady Wakefield had an affair..." He broke off, realizing what he would say next.

Thornton gave him a quizzical look as Blakesley continued. "Lady Wakefield could not have children after Richard. His birth was difficult, and her doctors advised against any more children, as they had their heir. They had a true love match, and so, Lady Wakefield encouraged her husband to set up a woman to slake his physical needs. There was a widow nearby who agreed to the arrangement, and she was Lady Lucilla's mother."

Aubrey thought about the late Lady Wakefield. She had been a slender blond woman, gracious and kind to him and loving to Lucy. There had been no sign she was not Lucy's real mother though there was not much resemblance between them. Lucy had often remarked that she was the changeling in her family and that she fit much closer to the Lovell family though she and Aubrey had different eyes. Aubrey's eyes were a startling golden color while Lucilla had dark brown chocolate eyes. Their hair was almost the same although days spent in the Italian sun had tipped Aubrey's hair with gold.

Thornton took up the story. "The pleasant widow died giving birth, and Lady Wakefield took the child and raised her as her own daughter."

"How did I not know this?" Aubrey wondered aloud. "We are their neighbors. Surely there would have been gossip in the parish."

"I believe the family was very discreet, seeing no need to brunt the news about. And it wasn't as if the girl would inherit. Lord Wakefield took good care of her, she has a dowry designed to attract the lowest of fortune hunters."

"You said there was a scandal in her first season?" Aubrey probed trying to act casual. He took another sip of his brandy, hoping he was fooling Thornton. The others were too embroiled in their own arguments to concern themselves with his interest, but Thornton had a fine mind and took in far more than people realized.

Blakesley sniffed but was the first to answer him. "There was a problem with her first season, and it delayed her come-out. I believe there was an illness, and then Lord Wakefield and then his wife died, so Lady Lucilla did not make her debut until she was almost twenty. Richard had his hands full with his new responsibilities and brought a great-aunt to chaperone her, but the old woman was careless. Lady Lucilla was a little wild, perhaps because she was older for her first Season, and some gossips caught her alone in a garden with Rathburn."

Aversley interrupted, "He is a confirmed rake just after her dowry. The lady was correct to refuse him, despite what the Ton thought."

"He made an offer, and she turned him down?" To Aubrey, that was unheard of. "But what of her family? Didn't they insist on a wedding?" It would have been very unusual in their society for there not to be a wedding if a man compromised a young lady. There should have been no choice for Lucy.

"Richard did not insist, despite Rathburn's claim he had compromised the lady. Lady Lucilla retired to the country and has only been back for short trips since then," Thornton replied quietly. "Her family seems to allow her a remarkable degree of laxity in her behavior, but perhaps they realize that they can do nothing else at this point."

"Rathburn insisted she had succumbed to his advances and was furious when she turned him down." Blakeley seemed to find this amusing and Aubrey clenched his fist under the table, wanting to smash in his smug face, even if he was one of his oldest friends.

"Yes, well, he did not want to lose her fortune, and it did not do his own reputation any good for having her refuse him." Aversley looked like thunder and Blakesley seemed to realize that the Lady Lucilla was a good friend to the Lady Harriet.

"Her brother went to school with James Lennox and my brother. Carlisle has taken her under his wing and escorts her when she is in town. She has dispensed with a chaperone mostly and acts more like a widow than an unmarried woman." Thornton gave a pointed look at Blakesley, and he slunk even further down in his chair. "I like her. She has a great deal of common sense and keeps to herself when she's in town. She's not invited to most of the social affairs unless Carlisle brings her, which is a shame. I'm glad Lady Harriet has continued to stand by her friend." Thornton gave a nod to Aversley.

Aubrey sat back, his body rigid and his mind in a whirl. The others had changed subjects and were discussing the horses at Tattersalls, ignoring him. For the first time in five years, he felt hope, just the tiniest little ray, but it was hope.

Chapter Four

Lady Lucy Blount was restless, staring out the back window of the drawing room into the garden. She had already walked in the park, not as much as she did at home, but still, it was better than sitting here. One of her favorite activities was to read, and Lucy had several new books to choose from her shopping trip with Harriet. But she could not seem to settle.

It was all Aubrey's fault. She would never have come to town, wedding or no if she had known what Aubrey would do when she saw him again. Well, she was not sure what she wanted him to do, but the cool demeanor, the unruffled calm had infuriated her. Five years and all he could do was drawl in that affected tone and pretend at an introduction as if he did not know her.

She tapped her finger on the window pane and sighed. Harriet was so cross with her. To have made such a scene in public could lead to such a scandal it would eclipse Harriet's and Aversley's wedding. Harriet had taken an enormous risk in asking her to be a participant, and this was how she had returned the favor. But Harriet would not let her return home either.

Lucy drew her hand away and rubbed at the bruise that had formed from her unexpected fisticuffs. She hoped Aubrey had a similar bruise on his cheek. Maybe that would remind him who she was and how he knew her.

She wanted to go home, to the dales of Yorkshire. She hated the city, the cruel Ton members who scorned her, gossiped about her and laughed at her when they did not know her at all. If it were not for Harriet, she would already be in a coach heading north.

Harriet had scolded her once they had reached the carriage. A lady did not indulge her temper in that manner at any time, but especially in public. How could she? And what had Viscount Lovell done anyway that merited such behavior?

Lucy had calmed down by that time and that she had behaved in such a way mortified her. It would have been better to treat him with icy disdain.

She had apologized to Harriet and begged her to let her go home. Her presence would only ruin Harriet's wedding, and Lucy loved her friend too dearly to allow that to happen. But Harriet had been fierce and refused to permit any retreat.

"I do not understand why you behaved so and you will not explain why you bear such a grudge against Lord Lovell. He was not even in London during your Season. But he and George are the best of friends, having attended school together. So it is unfortunate you are both standing up for us, but you will be civil and behave, at least until after the wedding." Harriet was adamant.

"I am so sorry, Harriet. It was bad behavior on my part, going back to our childhood." Lucy felt remorseful, especially when confronted with Harriet's embarrassment and indignation. "I'm sure I should return home and let this scandal die a natural death. If I leave now, you'll have time before the wedding for everyone to forget this incident even happened."

"No, you are not going anywhere," Harriet had said emphasizing her order with a sharp tap on Lucy's hand. "You will be in my wedding party. And we will put this behind us." She had rested her finger on her lips, tapping as she thought.

"I have it," she had exclaimed. "You will attend the theater tonight with George, Lovell, and me. You will be nice to him, and everyone will see that the incident just now was an unfortunate misunderstanding.

And from now on at the events we attend, you must dance or even flirt with him." By this time the carriage had stopped, and Harriet had fixed Lucy with a gimlet stare.

"I can't attend tonight, Harriet. I promised Carlisle that I would attend the Etherington's musicale with him. You know he must leave in the morning for a few days at his estate, and I cannot let him down. But you have a good plan. From now on I will attend whatever you wish." Lucy had promised, caught by her friend's tears and dismay.

She bit her lower lip, thinking about her deceit. Carlisle had already left for his estates, so Lucy was staying at home this evening. Harriet would be furious when she found out, but Lucy couldn't bear facing Aubrey again so soon.

She leaned forward, resting her forehead against the pane of glass as she gazed out at the small garden in the townhouse's back. Aubrey had looked well. The gangly youth had been replaced by a lean man with darkened skin and chestnut hair lightened by the sun. His face didn't have the easy humor he had had as a young man but seemed more serious. Of course, he had been tense, seeing her for the first time in all these years. He must feel guilt for the way he had treated her.

For a long time, Lucy had thought Aubrey had left without the least care in the world. One day he would marry her and then the next day he disappeared, out of the country, without leaving a note or any word of explanation. She had believed his protestations of love and loved him in return, with all the fervor of a young girl. Lucy had given him her innocence, and he had betrayed her, all because she was not born with the proper bloodlines.

She had been raised as a lady but had found out shortly after Aubrey left her that her mother, Lady Sybil, and the woman who had raised her, was not her blood mother. She had adopted Lucy at birth. Lucy didn't mind; Lady Sybil would always be her real mama as she didn't even know the woman who had birthed her. Lady Sybil had explained, and Lucy had hugged her, and they had cried together. She had loved her as her daughter, and Lucy had been distraught at her death.

But what had most hurt her was that Aubrey St Clare would perceive her as less because her mother was not a lady. That he could see her as so inconsequential that he would seduce her with promises of marriage and then abandon her once he'd had her. Oh, she had been naïve, and that innocence had led her astray.

Her first and only Season had been awful. Her father's death had delayed it, and then Lady Sybil's death had followed. She had not wanted to leave Wakefield Hall, but Richard had insisted. He promised her she needed to go to London and enjoy herself with all the activities that a young lady of the Ton would relish.

But it had been a disaster. Aside from Harriet, she had found no friends among the young women. Most were younger than her, silly in their innocence and youth. And only her fortune or her looks had interested the men. Once the rumors of her birth had surfaced, it had been her possible lack of morals from being illegitimate that had attracted the men. Any of the respectable men who might have offered marriage drifted away. She didn't want a marriage offer, but she had promised Richard that she would try.

The fortune hunters, the rakes and the dissolute, men who wanted her dowry or her body was all who remained. Then had come the reckless night when she had let Rathburn take her into the garden at the Remington's ball. No one had danced with her, and she was angry and bored. She had not cared about the matrons who eyed her askance. Her Great-aunt Sylvia had disappeared into the card room, and Rathburn had appeared with a glass of punch, charming her and leading her into the garden.

He had stolen a kiss and Lucy had allowed it, curious to see how it felt to kiss someone other than Aubrey. But of course, someone had caught them, Rathburn had proposed, and she had just as quickly refused him. It was stupid to have to marry a man just because he had kissed her, and she had no feelings except loathing for Rathburn. He apparently had feelings for her dowry because he had tried to insist. Richard had sided with her, but it had caused a terrible scandal. Gossip abounded that it had been more than a kiss and everyone except for Harriet had refused to associate with her.

Richard had allowed her to return home, much to her relief. Harriet had remained her friend, and they corresponded, confiding in each other. Lucy had been glad for her when Aversley took an interest that developed into real feelings on both sides. Harriet was a good woman and deserved happiness.

So, Lucy was glad for her friend and, though she hated leaving Yorkshire, had taken the long journey to London to help Harriet celebrate her nuptials with Aversley. Richard could not accompany her as Anne, his wife, was carrying their first child. So he had insisted that Carlisle would escort Lucy and watch over her in Town.

Carlisle was an old friend of his from his school days. Lucy knew he liked her, and she liked him in return and enjoyed his company, but she had been right to refuse his marriage proposal. He was not in love with her, but he needed a wife and was being protective of her. But she did not need protection, not from any man. She had learned at a young age to protect her heart, and she would never fall in love again.

The door to the drawing room opened and the housekeeper, Mrs. Brundage, stood there.

"My lady, would you like tea?" she inquired.

Lucy shook her head. The townhouse had the minimal staff as Richard thought that she was staying with Harriet. Lucy preferred being alone.

"Thank you, Mrs. Brundage, but I would prefer a supper tray in my room a little later. Whatever you have on hand is fine. I will stay in tonight."

"Yes, my lady," Mrs. Brundage curtseyed and left.

Lucilla turned back to the window and sighed. Aubrey being here undoubtedly complicated things. Well, she would be polite and otherwise ignore him. He had ignored her for the last five years, so presumably, he was no more anxious to be with her now. And it was only for a few weeks.

She reached into her pocket and pulled out the miniature she had slipped into it earlier when she had returned to the house. It was a picture of her painted when she was seventeen, her hair flowing down her back, thick and unruly, and the glow of first love on her face. Aubrey had done it, and she had treasured it when he gave it to her. Now she kept it to remember his betrayal.

Her resolve firmed, and she nodded to herself, determined to get through the next days with poise and grace. He would not take her unawares again.

Chapter Five

Aubrey strode into his front entryway, dropping his hat and gloves on the table before the footman even reached him. He had spent the evening at home, begging off from his invitation to the theater with Aversley, and had indulged in a little too much brandy after leaving the club. An early morning ride had cleared his head, and now he was eager to find his mother.

He reached the breakfast room, but it was empty. His mother had been out the previous evening, and he had missed her at dinner, so he had sat in his library and brooded.

The footman had caught up with him and put together a plate of food for his breakfast from the dishes on the sideboard. Aubrey might have missed English breakfasts most of all during his sojourn in Italy. He took a bite of cold veal pie and sipped at his tea. There was nothing like English tea. Even if not grown in England, it seemed to taste differently here in England — maybe it was the cream.

Aubrey shook his head, wondering at his wandering thoughts. He glanced at the doorway, but it was too early for his mother to be up and about yet. He grimaced to himself, the questions he wanted to pose to her running through his mind again.

"Is everything to your liking, my lord," the footman had noticed his frown.

"This is fine," he replied. "Has my mother arisen yet?"

"No, her ladyship rarely appears for some time yet, unless she plans to attend an event during the day." The footman bowed and backed away into a corner.

Aubrey nodded absently and drummed his fingers on the table. He unrolled the newspaper that sat on the corner of the table and pretended to read it, but his mind was far away again.

He had rushed into his mother's drawing room where she was sitting with some needlework, her head bent over the frame as her slender fingers pulled the crimson thread through the cloth. Her dark hair was prematurely shot through with gray, and he paused for a moment, watching her and hoping that she might find happiness in the news he brought. She had so little joy in her life. Aubrey's father was a bluff, jovial man, but seldom at home. He would rather spend his time with friends, gambling or hunting, then home with his brittle wife. And he had many other women he would consort with and did not care if his wife or heir knew of his affairs.

She looked up her lips tight. "Slowly, my son, slowly. Behave like a gentleman, there is no need to rush about," she rebuked him.

"Yes, mother." He had gone to sit at her side. She had glanced at him, curious, but turned back to her embroidery.

"Mother, I have news." Aubrey bit his lip, but she still did not look at him. He took a big gulp of air and laid his hands on his knees, waiting for her to acknowledge him.

She finished the stitch and placed her needlework in her lap. She looked at her son, her lips pursed and eyes narrowed. If only he could please her, he would do anything. But he had learned long ago that he could not control her happiness.

"Yes, Lovell, what is it?" She never called him by his name, never touched him. Lady Lovell stayed remote and cold to everyone around her, treating servants and her son alike.

"I am to be married." Her eyes widened, and her lips tightened, but she did not respond otherwise.

Aubrey continued, watching her. "Lady Lucilla has consented to be my bride. We are to be married as soon as it can be arranged."

"No."

Aubrey started, sure he had not heard her, her voice had been so soft.

"You may not marry Lady Lucilla Blount. You are both too young."

"I am a man now, mother. I have finished university and will take on the duties of the estate, helping father. And Lady Lucilla does not want a season, anyway. There is no need to delay."

His mother clenched her hands together, the knuckles turned white. "No, you do not understand. You may not marry Lady Lucilla."

"You are correct, I do not understand. We are in love, and it is a good match. She is the daughter of an Earl and..."

His mother interrupted with a harsh laugh, her mouth tilted up to one side in a sneer. "She is no Earl's daughter. Lucilla is the daughter of a Viscount." She stood and crossed to the front of the fireplace, then turned back to face him.

"Lady Wakefield was one of your father's paramours," she said bitterly. "Lady Lucilla Blount is your sister."

The room spun around Aubrey, and his stomach roiled. "No, no, that cannot be. Lady Wakefield is devoted to her husband. My father would never..." But he stopped, knowing his father would if he had the opportunity.

He closed his eyes and leaned back against the sofa. True, he and Lucy had the same coloring, different from her brother, Richard, but he had thought nothing of that. Oh, God, he and Lucilla had... but that intimacy was a grave sin, even if they did not know. Aubrey stood and staggered to a corner where he cast up his accounts, all over his mother's prize Aubusson rug.

His mother stood with her hands folded at her waist, watching him, until he finished emptying his stomach. He wiped the back of his hand against his mouth, tasting the bitterness and the bile.

He had gone to Italy the next morning without leaving word for either of his parents or Lucy. It was better she thought him a cad who had toyed with her affections and taken her innocence then she knew the truth.

Where was his mother? He was impatient to confront her. At the time, he'd believed her story. There was no reason for her to lie and what she said was plausible, except that he knew in his heart that Lady Wakefield would never betray her husband. The differences between his parents' relationship and Lucy's parents loving affection was night and day.

If the story that Blakesley had told him was true, then he had left for naught. He and Lucy might have married. Aubrey should have waited, investigated further, asked his father. He had never stopped loving Lucy, and now she hated him. Aubrey put that thought aside. He would resolve that matter later once he had confirmed Blakesley's story with his mother.

He pushed away from the table, intent on finding his mother. Aubrey thought he might burst out of his skin if he did not talk to her directly. He strode down the parquet floors to the stairway. His boots clicked on the steps as he took them two at a time to the second floor. He knocked on his mother's door and waited. Surely she was up by now.

"Yes," Aubrey heard from within the room.

"I wondered if I might have a word," he called.

"Come in."

Aubrey turned the doorknob and entered the room. It was an ample space, done in cream and crimson with touches of gold. Someone had pulled the curtains back and French, his mother's maid, was bustling about, clothing in her hands. His mother sat in bed, a tray on her lap, taking a sip of her favorite chocolate. Aubrey stopped and studied her. She was a thin woman, her hair pulled back severely, her face unlined, one eyebrow raised as she looked up at him.

"Yes, Lovell, what is it?" the dowager Lady Lovell put her cup down and waited.

Aubrey glanced at French, and she curtseyed and disappeared into the dressing room. His mother put her cup down and crossed her hands in her lap, waiting for him to speak. Aubrey thought her foot would tap if she had been standing.

"I met Lady Lucilla Blount yesterday when I was doing errands." Best to be direct, Aubrey thought.

His mother's lips tightened into a sneer. "There was gossip at Remington's soiree last evening. I understand there was an incident." She picked her cup up again, but Aubrey saw her hand tremble, just a little. "She should not have involved you. Bad breeding there." She sniffed and narrowed her eyes at him.

"I couldn't avoid it, Mother." Aubrey realized he was getting off track. "But there was talk at my club afterward. Interesting talk." He realized that he had clenched his fists, his whole body tense. He deliberately relaxed, knowing she would recognize his tension and take advantage.

She sipped her chocolate, her eyes studying him over the rim. Lady Lovell was an old adversary, and Aubrey needed to be careful. She was so much better at this than he was.

"I supposed you would like to hear what the gossip was at my club?"

"No, I don't care for gossip."

"It was about her parentage." Aubrey drew in a deep breath and waited.

Another sniff and his mother put the cup back down on the tray with a rattle. She picked up a biscuit, breaking off a small piece and brought it to her lips.

"Mother, why did you tell me she was my half-sister?"

"Did I?" She did not look up, just studied the piece of biscuit.

Aubrey held on to his temper. "Yes, you did. But she's not, that was never true." He clenched his fists again, but this time, he did not relax them. "Why would you tell me that?"

"Oh, Aubrey, what does it matter now? It is over and done with." She sighed and looked up at him. "You were too young, and Lady

Lucilla was not good enough for you, but you were infatuated with her. I did not mean for you to run away to Italy though."

"No, mother, it is not over and done with." Aubrey strode to the window and looked out, wanting to put his fist through the glass. Five years gone by, he thought, five years lost.

"Lovell, you are making too much of this," his mother sounded nervous. "You have moved on, the girl, I presume, has moved on so what is the difference now?"

Aubrey whirled around. "What is the difference? Five years I lost with the woman I love."

Lady Lovell's eyes widened, but she attempted to regain the upper hand. "Lovell, you are acting like a child deprived of his favorite toy. We do not marry for love, but for money or status. From what I hear, you can have the girl as your mistress. Meanwhile, I can look for a suitable wife for you, now you have returned home. I had already thought of a few young ladies of appropriate rank...." Her voice trailed off as she took in the look on his face. Aubrey had never been one to put on appearances as many of the Ton did, but his face had turned to stone, a mask she could not penetrate.

"I think you have said and done enough. I would like you out of the house. Perhaps your sister would be amenable to a visit, but I do not care where you go. I want you out of my affairs," as he strode towards the door, he tossed back over his shoulder, "Immediately."

He stood trembling outside his mother's door and closed his eyes for a moment, trying to decide what to do next. Scattered thoughts and visions ran through his mind, and he rolled his shoulders, attempting to loosen the tension there.

He walked down the hall to the room at the back he used as a studio. It was well lit, suitable for his painting. He had had the carpet removed, and his easel stood ready for him to work, but he was not in the mood to put brush to canvas now. He walked over to a stack of paintings piled up against the wall and went through them, pulling them out one by one. The first few were landscapes, views of the Tuscan hills or the sparkling waters of the Mediterranean Sea. Then he reached the portraits and Aubrey took them and placed them in a row against the wall, displaying them to his view.

They were all the same person, a young girl with chestnut hair and laughing brown eyes. Two were formal poses, but the rest showed her in more natural settings, picking wildflowers or picnicking on a lawn. Another showed her sitting on a tree branch, laughing, with dainty toes just peeking from under the hem of her dress.

The last portrait showed her laying on a robe in the grass, her eyes languorous and her mouth in a sweet smile. She was nude, pink nipples peeking out from between long chestnut curls. One arm trailed over her hip, her dainty hand covering the chestnut curls at the juncture of her thighs. Aubrey squatted in front of it, studying the face that had haunted his dreams, sleeping and waking. He reached out and caressed the cheek as if he could feel her soft skin under his fingertip once again.

He stood back up and wandered over to his easel. His latest portrait was half-finished and was of Lucilla as she stood in the ballroom the evening when he had first seen her again. Her peach dress glowed in the candlelight, and she had her hair piled up on her head. He wished that she was here standing before him. Aside from one miniature he had done for her, he had painted all the portraits from memory. But it would be glorious to have her sit for him again, the easy banter between them while he painted until he had to kiss her plump lips, so soft and sweet.

Aubrey scratched at the scruff on his face as he realized the truth. There was no impediment between him and Lucy. Instead of lamenting the lost five years, he would create a new future for them. She might hate him now, but he would win her back. Whistling, he turned and left the room, ready for a bath and clean clothes. He had things to do.

Chapter Six

Lucy nervously smoothed the green silk of the evening gown she had chosen for this evening. It had a cream tulle overskirt and was one of her favorites. She would need all the encouragement she could get this evening.

Harriet sat beside her, pretty in a bright yellow dress that contrasted with her dark hair. Harriet was the type of woman who would become more striking as she aged. George sat across from them, smiling at his fiancée. They were so happy together despite the troubles that had preceded their engagement.

George's family thought George could do so much better than Harriet. They had sneered at Harriet's status as the poor daughter of the dissolute Earl of Brandwine. Harriet's father had gambled his estate away and caroused through London with nary a care for the hopes of his young daughter. An aunt had brought Harriet out for her Season, and Harriet and George had met and fallen in love almost at once. George's mother kept throwing other young ladies at him and had colluded in a scheme to compromise her son so he could not marry Harriet. But luck had intervened, and George had stood up to his mother and claimed Harriet for his own.

Harriet reached over and clasped Lucy's nervous fingers. "Be calm, my dear. This will all work out. My dear George has spoken to Lovell, and our plan is in place."

Lucy smiled apprehensively at her friend. She would do anything for Harriet, but she had argued against her plan strenuously. Only the thought she would need to face society for the next few weeks made her capitulate. The rumors were already flying about, making the incident even more exaggerated. George had heard someone say she had knocked Lovell out with a fist to his jaw. They needed to squelch the rumors at once.

She wished that Carlisle had not had to leave to take care of an estate matter. She would have liked to have him at her side tonight. There would be no tittering in the ballroom if he were there. And then perhaps she would not have to face Aubrey or be part of Harriet's scheme.

The carriage jolted to a halt, and Lucy straightened her spine, already girding for battle. Harriet gave her hand a quick squeeze, and then they prepared to follow George out of the carriage. He handed each of them down in front of the Roth's stairway. This would be a crush. People were already streaming up the stairs, past the huge baskets of flowers under the torchlight. A few women glanced at the new arrivals and then turned away when they recognized Lucy. The men were more inclined to leer, and Lucy suppressed the urge to roll her eyes.

George took Harriet on his arm and led them up the stairway. Lucy followed, but she noticed that while several people greeted the couple ahead of her, no one acknowledged her at all. She lifted her head a little higher. Lucy didn't care about any of them and couldn't wait until Harriet and George wed so she could return home. But Harriet's scheme meant that she would need to spend time with Aubrey just to show it was all just a misunderstanding. She set her lips. It was not a misunderstanding. She hated Lovell. Lucy must think of him as Lovell, not Aubrey. She would endure him with icy politeness and tolerate the next few weeks. They did not need to spend much time together, and once the wedding was over, she would never need to see him again.

The ballroom was crowded and overheated for this May evening despite the open doors at the back of the room. Couples whirled around the dance floor, and others stood in chattering groups where they could see and be seen. The poor wallflowers stood in scattered clumps, hemmed in by their anxious mamas while the chaperones and dowagers sat where they had the best vantage point. It was a typical London society event, and Lucy wanted to flee from the prying eyes and overly perfumed odors. She almost turned to leave, but Harriet glanced back over her shoulder to check on her, smiling although her eyes betrayed her worry.

Harriet's presence soothed Lucy although her friend did not seem as sure of her plan as she had earlier. She took a deep breath and smiled back, following them through the crowds.

George led them over to where his friend, the Earl of Thornton was surveying the crowds. Thornton was a reserved man but not unapproachable, and Lucy liked the little she knew of him, despite him being one of Aubrey's, rather Lovell's friends. He was dreadfully handsome, and all the young ladies swooned over him while their mamas swooned over his title and wealth. Lord Lovell, however, was indifferent to swooning and rarely attended events where young ladies might waylay him. Like Lucy, he was only here because of his friend's upcoming nuptials.

Thornton did not leer or give her the cut, but he eyed her with curiosity as George greeted him. Harriet gave her a nudge and Lucy remembered that he was also a part of the ploy to rehabilitate her. Harriet had made George enlist all his friends in the effort. Lucy sighed, foreseeing a long evening ahead. At least, Lovell did not appear to have arrived yet.

Thornton nodded his head acknowledging the ladies. "Good evening, Lady Harriet, Lady Lucilla. Quite the crush tonight. That so many attend her ball must delight Lady Roth." Lucy curtseyed and nodded, but did not bother to reply, leaving that courtesy to Harriet. She turned and surveyed the ballroom, trying to appear aloof and impervious to the stares. The thought of seeing Aubrey again overwhelmed her. Perhaps he would not come despite George's appeal.

He could be no more eager to see her again than she was to meet with him.

When George and Harriet excused themselves to dance, they left her alone with Thornton. "Would you like to dance?" he asked politely, holding out his hand to take hers. Lucy nodded her assent and Thornton led her out for a set of country dances. He was a graceful dancer, and Lucy was out of practice, so she concentrated on her footsteps, thankful that the dance did not allow for much conversation.

She was breathless and rosy from the warmth of the room and exertion of the dance when the set finished. Lovell gave her a brief smile but didn't talk to her as he led her back to where Harriet and George waited.

"Thank you, my lord, for the dance. I fear I am a trifle out of practice at the steps." Lovell nodded and walked away.

"Practicing your wiles again, my dear," a deep voice came from behind her, and she stiffened. The hot, hard body came up too close to her, and she tried to step away. He had hold of her arm and kept her pinned to his side in full view of anyone who might look in the ballroom.

The Earl of Rathburn chuckled when she hissed, "Let me go."

"I think not." his voice was velvet. "I have waited to see you return to society. We have unfinished business." His hot breath blew over her ear as he leaned in so no one else would hear and Lucy shivered in distaste. She lifted her dancing slipper and brought it down on his instep, trying to get him to release her without making more of a scene.

Harriet looked horrified, her plan going awry before her eyes. George's face looked determined as he stepped forward, but then he stopped and blew out a breath in relief.

Chapter Seven

"Please release the lady, Rathburn. I believe this is my dance." Lucy closed her eyes in equal parts relief and dismay that Aubrey had finally appeared. Rathburn hesitated, but then let go of her arm and stepped back.

"Lady Lucilla and I were just recalling old times." Rathburn tilted his chin, his eyes narrowed as he inspected the newcomer. "Pleasant times as I recollect, eh, my dear?"

Lucy shivered at the endearment. She wondered how she had ever thought Rathburn attractive. True, she had been in despair during her first season, and he seemed to be the only man interested in her. Lucy didn't know of his reputation or how he had gambled his wealth away, so he needed a wealthy heiress to wife. She had been naïve to think he could ever replace Aubrey in her affections and shocked when he displayed his true colors.

Lucilla opened her eyes to see Aubrey standing in front of her, his hand out as he claimed her for the dance. She stepped forward, all thought of her ill feelings for him disappearing in her haste to escape from Rathburn. He took her gloved hand, and a dart of heat ran up her arm. He apparently did not feel it as he pulled her forward to the dance floor. And of all the luck, it was a waltz that the orchestra played.

He took her in his arms, and another shiver ran through Lucy's body, but this time it was not from revulsion. She noticed the shocked glances from the people around them but did not have time to react as he whirled her away. They had never danced the waltz in their time together, only country dances at local parties. Lucy bit her lip, trying to collect herself and ignore the closeness of the hard male body holding her.

"I apologize if I interrupted a tête-à-tête, but I have only just arrived." His voice was brandy-smooth, just as she remembered and Lucy looked up to see his handsome face set. His eyes narrowed as he studied her. "Lady Harriet seemed to indicate that my presence was necessary now, not later as she had originally wished."

Lucy flushed, reminded that he was only here to help to dissipate the scandal she had caused. He had a small bruise on his face where she had hit him, and the urge to reach up and soothe the injury struck her. She tensed, wondering she had fallen back so fast into her old ways and gathered herself.

"Lord Rathburn is an old acquaintance, but not a welcome one. I appreciate your help in the matter, especially after the way I treated you yesterday." Lucy took a deep breath and continued. "My lord, I must apologize for my behavior yesterday. I mistook you for someone else and as a lady..." she faltered as his grip tightened.

"Lucy, you would never mistake me for anyone else. And I deserved that slap and more." His eyes glinted as her mouth dropped open in shock. When Harriet had come up with this mad scheme that Lovell escort her to several events until the gossip died down, Lucy had refused adamantly. Once Harriet had convinced her it was the only salvation of their reputations, she had agreed. She expected that Aubrey had only acceded because of George and that he would be as unwilling as her to be together. But he sounded sincere.

"You look lovely tonight," Aubrey said, and it was as if he had tipped a bucket of ice water over her. Lucy looked away, her gaze cool and her lips tight.

"What is the matter?" Aubrey had not missed the tenseness of her body. It was a delight to hold her so close again, breathing in her scent, and he feasted his eyes like a starving man at a banquet.

"I see you have not changed," Lucy's voice sounded stern. She kept her face turned away, and Aubrey pulled her a little closer, trying to gain her attention again.

"What does that mean?" Her attitude amused him. But Aubrey was so relieved to be holding her back in his arms he did not care if he irritated her right now. He had a lot to make up for and did not expect instant forgiveness. That she had gone along with the plan he had proposed to Harriet and George gave him some hope for eventual exoneration, but tonight was only the first step.

When he had seen Rathburn accosting her, he had raced across the room despite the original plan to dance with her later in the evening. Aubrey had remained calm though he would not speak to the outcome if Rathburn had not released her so fast. Aubrey would have made an even greater scandal in that case. But the fact he had come to her rescue would confuse the gossips and mollify any further rumors.

Lucy shrugged and did not answer him, but tried to pull away and put a little more distance between them. He held her against him, and she looked up, her eyes glittering with anger.

"My lord, please, this is unseemly," she hissed.

"Yet we have been closer than this," he whispered back, and it pleased him to see the blush creep up her neck. Her eyes narrowed, and she tried to pull a hand away from him.

"No, no, Lucy." He was laughing, so giddy to hold her in his arms again. "No hitting me again, even if I deserve it."

She glared and looked away, determined not to give him any further reaction. It hurt her to the heart to see Aubrey laughing and so pleased with himself after all this time. She had hoped that he had spent the last five year in misery jend instead he had not a care in the world.

"Where did this sudden propensity for hitting come from, anyway? I don't recall a partiality for bodily harm from you in the past." He was teasing her.

"Perhaps I have been hitting every gentleman I have met in the last five years. How would you know?" She was proud her attitude was so nonchalant.

He sobered instantly. "I would not blame you if you took me as an example of a gentleman."

She looked up again as he swept her past another couple. "Why all the apologies, Lord Lovell? You have no reason for regret."

He almost stumbled. "Ah, Lucy, I have all the regrets in the world."

She tried to pull away again, her lips pressed together and two hot flashes of color on each cheekbone. He would not let her go, but Aubrey realized that he needed to rein in his blithe spirits. He was sincere, but she had no way to know that. She only knew he had left without a word of explanation and it was late in the day to clarify his actions. It would be better to act casually and gradually work his way back into her good graces.

"And how is your brother? I heard he had married," Aubrey thought to change the topic, but he winced, feeling he should not have mentioned marriage.

Lucy was not so sensitive. "He is well. He married Lady Anne Grey, daughter of the Earl of Warwick. They are awaiting their first child. Otherwise, they would have accompanied me to Town." Lucy seemed to have calmed and was looking about the ballroom as they danced. Aubrey could not detect any more temper or animosity.

"And you are staying with Lady Harriet until the wedding?" This was inquisitive and personal, but Aubrey wanted to keep her talking.

"No, I am not."

"Are you staying at Richard's townhouse then?" Aubrey was over the line now, but he wondered about her. Lucy did not seem to have a chaperone, and it would be a scandal for her to be staying at the townhouse on her own. But Wakefield's townhouse was next to his own, and he had noticed no activity. The knocker was still off the door.

"It is none of your business, my lord." Lucy was avoiding an answer, and Aubrey moved on. She had piqued his curiosity, but he could take the subject up with George later. Meanwhile, he wanted to enjoy the sensation of holding Lucy in his arms once again.

"I am suitably chastised, Lady Lucilla." She looked up, surprised at his teasing tone, then rolled her eyes and looked away. He cleared his throat and tried again. "I understand that we are to go riding tomorrow. Aversley says he will provide a mount for you."

She licked her lips nervously, and a bolt of lust so intense hit Aubrey that he almost leaned down to trace her lips with his own tongue. He straightened and tried to regain control of his unruly body. Lucy did not seem to notice but continued to dance, still looking around the room.

"Yes, Harriet spoke to me already. I suppose there is no help for it." She sounded bitter, and Aubrey's lust pivoted to dismay.

"Lady Harriet's plan is good, Lucy, and it will help the gossip mongers move on to something else. Though I think you should try smiling at me, even if you don't want to." Aubrey gave her waist a little squeeze and pasted a gentle smile on his face.

"Don't cozen me, my lord." But Lucy gave him a smile even if it looked brittle. "And I did not give you leave to address me by given name."

"Lady Lucilla, I know better than to pull the wool over your eyes. I thought only to remind you of our goal here." Aubrey's face became serious. "Aversley is my friend, and I want him and Lady Harriet to be happy. And that includes not causing a scandal before their wedding day. We were good friends once, Lady Lucilla, and I would hope we can be friends once again, for the sake of our mutual friends if nothing else.

Lucy stiffened, chastened by his words, but nodded her head in agreement. The music ended, and Aubrey led her to the side of the room where George and Harriet waited. Harriet seized her hand and gave it a squeeze. "How wonderful to be all together," she said. She turned to Aubrey, giving him an arched eyebrow as if she were an actress waiting for her next line.

"This is a memorable night," Aubrey dutifully replied while Lucy rolled her eyes, looking out at the couples dancing by. Harriet gave George a subtle nudge, and he looked startled.

"I say, oh, yes, indeed," George harrumphed. Aubrey looked over at Lucy as she looked out across the room, her body tense as if she itched to get away from him. Harriet gave George another nudge and rolled her eyes toward Lucy. George started but understood her unspoken sign.

"Lady Lucilla, please give me the honor of leading you out for the next set of dances?" George gave a little bow while Harriet nodded at his good manners if not his willingness to agree to his fiancée's desires.

Lucy turned and smiled at George, ignoring Aubrey, and held out her hand for him to lead her out on the floor. Harriet watched, smiling fondly at Aversley, and then turned to Aubrey, taking his arm.

"I believe a stroll outside might be acceptable, my lord," she said. "It is so warm in here."

Aubrey nodded his head in agreement and led her to the open doors that led outside. Lady Harriet was a real general, marshaling her troops and making her plans. So far, her strategy was right on target. She had brought Lucy into his sphere without questioning her motives.

Aubrey led Lady Harriet off to the side of the terrace where they could still see into the ballroom. Only a few others were outside, and they were further out in the dark, away from the light of the torches and the ballroom.

Harriet turned and faced Aubrey, her arms crossed over her chest. "Now, my lord, you will tell me your intentions." She pushed a wayward curl back behind her ear, her body almost quivering as she stared up at Aubrey, squinting in the dim light.

"My intentions?" Aubrey parroted. "Lady Harriet, my intentions are only good towards Lady Lucilla." He held both hands out, palms up as if his intentions were in his hands for her to inspect.

Harriet sniffed, but her body relaxed, and she peered into the glass windows of the ballroom as if she could see George and Lucy dancing in the throng.

"Lucy is my friend. She stood by me when others jeered at the presumption inherent in my falling in love with Aversley. I would not put her in harm's way, my lord."

"Neither would I, Lady Harriet." Aubrey did not want to tip his hand, but he would assuage Lady Harriet's ruffled sensibilities. "I am looking for a wife, and Lady Lucilla's brother's lands are next to my own. It could be a good alliance for us both."

Harriet's eyes narrowed. "An alliance, my lord? That is all you are looking for?"

"Perhaps more," Aubrey murmured. "But it's up to Lucy."

Harriet noticed that he called Lucy by her familiar name, but did not mention it. Instead, she said, "A man hurt Lucy badly, and then other men, members of the Ton, have tried to take advantage of her. I would not see her hurt again. She is content with her life in the country, but maybe not happy."

Aubrey stiffened, bothered by what Harriet said. He spoke before he realized what he would say. "I would see her happy."

Harriet stepped back, a grin on her face. "Then we are in agreement, Lord Lovell." She took his arm, tugging him along. "Let us go back in. I want to find Aversley and dance again, unfashionable as that may be."

Chapter Eight

The next morning had a brisk breeze but was sunny. Lucy waited with Harriet on the steps in front of her home dressed in a dark red riding habit. Harriet was in blue, her cheeks flushed and looking pretty. She was also nervous.

"You know I am not much of a rider, Lucy," she said. "I cannot ride at a gallop. And I don't want to fall off and have an injury before my wedding."

"We'll take it slow. I'm sure that George has got us two slugs to ride and if the men want to go faster, I will stay with you."

Harriet grimaced, uncomfortable at her lack of riding skills. "It's just as well that George does not love me for my ability on a horse. But you are such a good rider. I do not wish to hold you back. Stay with Lovell as George does not mind riding with me."

Now it was Lucy's turn to grimace, but she did not reply. Growing up in the country as she had, she was an excellent rider. She and Aubrey had roamed the fields of the Yorkshire, often sneaking away together. Her father had given her a beautiful chestnut mare, dainty and skittish, but Lucy had loved her and named her Ophelia. She would ride for hours. Her family hadn't worried. Most times she had a groom with her and otherwise stayed on their own land.

But those times were long ago, and this was different. Lucy had gone along with Harriet's scheme last night, but there was no need for the playacting to extend much farther. She had slept fitfully, plagued with dreams of Aubrey's firm body and hot hands. There were dark crescents under her eyes, and Lucy told herself that it did not matter.

She would ride next to Harriet and Lovell could go to the devil. She would not let that bloody rake disturb her nights anymore. Lucy had put thoughts of him away years ago. She would plod on her horse next to Harriet no matter what anyone said.

Lucy could still feel the burn of Aubrey's hand on her waist and the heat of his body as he held her close when dancing the night before. She still breathed in his scent around her, the bergamot and faint male scent that signified only Aubrey. Damn the man, why couldn't he leave her alone? True, she had started this by impulsively slapping him on the street, but they must have appeased the gossips in the Ton by now. He had danced with her twice last night and then had led her into supper. He had attended her markedly, and Harriet had heard ridiculous rumors of a lover's quarrel they had smoothed over. The gossips must have moved on to someone new by now.

Although when Lucy had suggested this, Harriet had actually tut-tutted her. "No, no," she had been emphatic. Lucy must continue to suffer Aubrey's attention until the wedding had taken place. Lucy thought even Aubrey wouldn't wish to waste his time with her for another few weeks.

It would be better if Carlisle had returned, but his estate business still delayed him. He would distract her from Lovell until she could return home - if the Duke ever returned to London.

"Ah, here they are," Harriet exclaimed and Lucy looked up to see George and Aubrey approaching on horseback. A groom led two riding horses behind them. One horse was as Lucy had expected, steady and broad, a sedate companion for Harriet. But the other was a lovely mare that brought back memories of Ophelia, dark with white stockings, frisking her tail as she pulled at the leading rein.

The men dismounted to help the women onto their mounts. "Good morning, ladies." George was all good bonhomie this morning. "I trust you slept well," he addressed Harriet as she beamed a big smile at him and nodded.

Meanwhile, Aubrey approached Lucy and took her hand, a twinkle in his golden eyes as he noted her resistance. "A good morning to you, Lady Lucilla. You look lovely as always." He gave her hand a subtle squeeze while studying her face. In fact, Lucy looked tired and pale, dark circles under her eyes. She did not smile at his overture nor reply, her eyes darting to the mare as she tugged her fingers away from him. His smile faded and his lips tightened, but he gave no other sign that her indifference affected him.

"Let me help you up onto your mount, my lady." Lucy looked up then, startled, and turned to look for a mounting block or step she could use instead. Aubrey put his hands on her waist and lifted her as her head snapped back around, her eyes wide and her mouth round in surprise as her rump landed on the saddle. Aubrey ignored her, instead putting her boot into the stirrup and pulling the hem of her red habit down over it. Lucy fussed with the reins, trying to ignore the hot imprint of his hands on her waist.

Aubrey turned to remount his own stallion, a feisty chestnut named Seraph, a grin on his face and his mood restored. He had noted Lucy's discomfort at his touch which meant that his closeness affected her and that was all in his favor. Meanwhile, George had helped Lady Harriet onto her horse, and they were ready to set out. Lucy maneuvered to ride next to Harriet, leaving the two gentlemen to ride together. Aubrey casually moved Seraph in front of her, blocking her until George was next to Harriet. Lucy slanted her eyes and shot him a quick look, but followed Aubrey as they rode to the park. She looked all around her, refusing to acknowledge Aubrey on the horse next to her.

"It's a beautiful day for a ride." Aubrey drew her attention. Lucy continued to ignore him, studiously examining the front doors of the townhouse they were passing. "Do you not agree that it is a lovely day, Lady Lucilla?"

She turned her face towards him, eyes narrowed and lips pursed. "I suppose it is," she said, deciding that it was better to humor him.

"I thought when we reach the park, you might care for a gallop. Aversley will attend Lady Harriet."

"Perhaps I can stay with Lady Harriet, and you might gallop off with Lord Aversley." Lucy's tone was sickly sweet, but Aubrey ignored it.

"I remember how you used to ride at Wakefield, racing across the fields, your hair streaming out behind you. You loved to race your horse."

Lucilla felt his words like a blow to the pit of her stomach. Her face stiffened, and she stared straight ahead as she replied, "Perhaps at one time I was careless with my mount, but I have learned to pick more carefully. I am much more sedate now and not willing to take risky chances anymore." She turned her face towards him. "Those days are long gone. I do not remember them any longer."

Aubrey did not betray the clenching in his gut that her words caused, but gave a slight nod, acknowledging that he understood the meaning behind her speech. "You were never careless, Lucy, but perhaps it was I that was irresponsible and reckless. You can inspire a man to that. But I never meant for things to end how they did. Believe me when I say I was duped most cruelly. Otherwise, I would never have left you."

Lucy's face paled more, and she tensed in her saddle. "It matters naught anymore and never did. A harmless flirtation between two young people was all it was." She bit her lip and looked away.

"No, Lucy, it was never a flirtation, and not harmless. I believe I did great harm, and I'd like to make recompense."

Two bright spots appeared on Lucilla's cheeks, and she swallowed, trying to regain her composure. Her eyes grew bright, and she blinked, trying to stop tears from falling.

"Lucy, I..." Aubrey wanted to pull her over onto the saddle in front of him and hold her, but they were nearing the entrance to the park.

"It is nothing, my lord." Lucy straightened her back her shoulders set, and head tilted away from him. She longed to break into a gallop and fly away, but instead bit her lower lip and regained her composure. Aubrey eyed her and sighed, knowing he could say no more. There were too many other people around, and he could not be any more indiscreet that he already had been.

They had to stop at the entrance to the park as more riders and carriages jostled to enter the gates. Aubrey shook his head, impatient at the delay. How did anyone expect to get in a good ride? This was not even the busy time as that was later in the day. He longed for Lovell Abbey, the open fields around his home and the clear, fresh air of the north. It had been a long time he had been home since the day he had left Lucy and gone to Italy. He at once missed it with a pang that took his breath away. He wanted, he needed to go home, clear out of the city and its crowds and its dirty air. But he would not go until he could take Lucy with him.

He followed George and Harriet into the park, and it opened a little. He glanced over at Lucy, silent and composed on her mare, the little red hat that matched her habit perched fetchingly atop her chestnut curls. Their progress was slow. Carriages clogged the drive and groups of people strode the pathways. A sunny morning in London drove people to the outdoors, and George and Lady Harriet knew so many people they must continuously stop to greet friends and acquaintances.

It seemed like they would never proceed, Lucy thought. She longed to move on, away from the gossip and stares of the members of the Ton, but they had paused again, to chat with another group of people who had been walking nearby. Lucy gritted her teeth as Harriet and George dismounted to speak with them. The groom took the leads of their horses while they strolled a little apart. Lovell was still on his horse, talking to three men who had ridden up to greet him. She looked around, desperate to get away and slid from her mount, tossing the reins to the hapless groom. No one noticed as she strode away on a nearby path.

Chapter Nine

Aubrey was conversing with Thornton and Blakesley, who had ridden up with another man, William Smythe, a friend from their club. Blakesley was grousing about the crowds.

"I told you we should have gone to Green Park. At least there we might have got in a gallop." The crowded grounds disgusted him.

Aubrey nodded, his mind on Lucy, knowing he was not likely to have any private speech with her under the circumstances. He sighed, seeing that George and Lady Harriet were still on the ground laughing with their acquaintances. Harriet was a timid rider and took any excuse to get off of her horse. They would stroll for a while. All at once he realized that Lucy was no longer on her horse and turned his head, looking for her on the ground. The groom noticed him looking and nodded at a path that led down to the Serpentine River. Aubrey excused himself from his friends, ignoring the wink that Thornton gave him. He nodded his thanks to the groom and dismounted, passing his reins to the unfortunate groom who was now holding onto five horses.

He skirted around a small group of ladies trying to draw his attention, intent on finding Lucy. It was much less crowded on this path, away from those who thronged the main thoroughfare. He could see the sparkle of water ahead as the walkway emerged along the water.

As he came around a corner, Aubrey stopped and grinned at the sight ahead of him. How like his Lucy! Her boots were lying on the ground, and she had looped her habit up over one arm. She was standing on a limb of a tree overlooking the path, reaching up to the next branch. A nursemaid and a young girl were standing nearby, their arms waving frantically as they implored her to be careful. He could see a small gray animal above her head she was reaching for with care. Aubrey moved until he was under her, just in case he needed to break her fall if the branch gave. He could see her trim ankles and her stockinged feet. Her back arched as she reached above her head, trying to coax the small creature, a kitten mewling piteously as it clung to the branch.

"Please be careful, my lady," the nursemaid begged. The little girl, a lovely thing with blonde hair and blue eyes still glistening with tears, was jumping up and down in excitement.

Lucy had got the kitten to release its claws from the branch and was cuddling it close to her, one arm looped around the tree. Aubrey judged that he could speak without startling her.

"Hand it to me, and then I will help you down," he said. Lucy just looked at him, aware that he had been there all along. She reached down with the kitten and placed it in his hand. The kitten latched onto his cuff, digging into the broadcloth of his riding jacket with sharp little talons. His valet would not be happy when Aubrey returned from this excursion.

Aubrey took the kitten over to the nursemaid who opened the lid of the basket that was lying by her feet.

"Oh, thank you, my lord, and my lady. I don't know what I would have done, but Mary would bring her pet." Mary was crouching down by the basket peering in at the kitten. Aubrey bent down next to her, aware that Lucy was still in the tree behind him.

"Well, Mary, Lady Lucilla has rescued your kitten. I think you owe her some thanks." The little girl stood up and with a careful gravity, curtseyed to both Aubrey and to Lucy, then charmed Aubrey by leaning forward and giving him a soft kiss on the cheek.

Lucy watched their interaction, pain shooting into her heart and clenching that poor organ in her chest. Aubrey was so kind to the child. The little girl adored him, crediting him for the rescue of her pet even if

Lucy had done most of the work. What if, but she shook her head and blinked away the sudden tears.

Aubrey smiled and then turned to Lucy to help her down. She supposed that she could have swung down without too much trouble, but since he was here, she would take advantage. There was a guilty part of her that longed to touch him, but Lucy ignored it. He lifted his arms and clasped her waist while she rested her hands on his broad shoulders. The smile left his face as he looked up at her and his eyes grew hot as he stared silently up at her face. Flustered, Lucy pushed off the branch a little too hard and ended up crushed against his chest. He caught her and let her slide down, her breasts rubbing against his hard torso. She caught her gasp by biting her lower lip and something flared in his eyes, fiery and scalding. Lucy realized that, at least for that moment, he still wanted her and a quiver started deep in her belly. His hands were burning at her waist as she hit the ground and he held her steady when she stumbled.

Lucy swallowed and stepped away as his hands fell from her. She bent and slipped on her half boots, then fussed at her riding habit, straightening the dishabille, not meeting his eyes. She glanced over at the maid and the young girl, kitten ensconced in its basket, but they were walking away, so there was no help there.

"Harriet must wonder where I have gone. And the horses..." she trailed off as she peeked up at Aubrey. He was smiling at her, the dimple at the corner of his mouth in evidence now. "What is it?" Lucy self-consciously patted her head, sure she had unkempt hair or her hat tilted over one ear. *That dimple*, she thought, *that is what got me into so much trouble years before.*

Aubrey reached out and pulled at a glossy curl that had come loose. "I have always loved your hair," he mused. "So wild and so revealing of your character." He gave the curl a gentle tug and then tucked it behind her ear.

It vexed Lucy. What right did he have to judge her or to pretend to know her? He had gone for five long years, larking about the Continent without a care or concern for her while she had been here enduring trial and heartbreak. She whirled and strode past him, back to where the others were waiting with the horses.

"Wait, Lucy!" Aubrey seized her arm, pulling her back, and the force turned her around, back into his arms. "What is the matter? What did I say?"

"Let me go," she said as she pulled against his grasp, and he released her. He wore a puzzled look, as if not sure why her mood had changed so suddenly and truth to tell, she was not sure why either. All at once, the whole situation tired her. Aubrey knew nothing of her life for the last few years. He had left her without ever saying why he had so changed his mind about her. Now he was back and pretending as if the last five years had never happened.

"Are you angry with me?" he asked, studying her face for some hint of her mood.

"I do not think of you at all, my lord," she replied, wanting to lash out. "Now let me go. I need to find Harriet."

Aubrey's lips tightened, and his face lost all expression. "I will escort you back, my lady." He placed her hand on his arm as if they had been strolling along the Serpentine.

"You *do* remember that we are putting on an appearance for Harriet's sake, do you not?" he drawled just before they reached the small group still chatting away. Lucy stiffened but made no other sign than a little nod.

"Good," he said, and he led her to the group of people gathered around Harriet and George discussing the wedding. There were a few curious glances, but most ignored her. Two young ladies pounced on Aubrey right away. Lucy pulled away, stepping back towards Harriet, who was standing with George and did not appear to notice her either.

All at once she had had enough. Lucy whirled, turning back to where the groom was waiting, holding onto the reins of the horses.

"My lady," he stammered as Lucy pulled her reins away. She paused for a moment, trying to decide what to do, but the groom had his hands full and could not help. She could not get into the saddle herself without a block or a leg up. Lucy wanted to stamp her booted foot. She thought about just walking away, leaving the horse, the people laughing and talking, Harriet, George, and above all, Aubrey de Vere.

"Lady Lucilla, is something amiss?" George had noticed her standing by her horse. "Are you in a hurry to go? Harriet has met old friends, but if you are in a rush, I can fetch her away."

"No, no, it's... I have a headache, that's all. I don't want to disturb Harriet." Lucy closed her eyes and leaned against the saddle, breathing in the soothing scent of horse and leather.

"I can take you back, or I can ask Lovell." George turned, but Lucy whirled and caught his arm before he could go any further.

"No, if you would just give me a leg up, I can return home while bothering no one."

"I do not think Harriet would approve of letting you ride home by yourself, a young lady on her own." George studied her face, startled by the desperation on Lucy's face. Something there convinced him, and he gave a sigh. "Very well, let me give you a leg up. Billy can go with you after he ties off the rest of the horses."

Lucy squeezed his arm. "Thank you so much, George. I'll be right as rain once I reach home. I appreciate your kindness."

George humphed and threw her up on her saddle, then said, "Be careful, my lady. Once you reach your townhouse, give Billy the mare and please take care of yourself. I'm sure that Harriet will be in touch later today."

She nodded and turned the mare, sneaking a look, but Aubrey had his back to her and did not appear to notice she was leaving. She urged her horse to a trot, followed by the groom.

Lucy disregarded the curious stares of the other riders and carriages as she passed through the gates. Her brother's townhouse was not far. Once she reached it, she did not even wait for poor Billy, but slid down, landing on the street with a jolt. She tossed her reins to the beleaguered groom, called her thanks, and hurried up the steps. She rushed in and slammed the door behind her, then relaxed the tenseness in her shoulders. This had been a bad idea to visit London. If only she'd known Aubrey had returned. She would not have come within a hundred miles of the city.

A creamy envelope on the side table in the hallway caught her attention. She picked it up and sighed when she saw the wax imprint for Carlisle. Jamie must have returned. She hoped that he would not continue to press her for marriage. Still, that gave her an idea. James Lennox, Duke of Carlisle, was a big man and could provide a suitable shield, at least for the next several days.

Chapter Ten

Aubrey tugged at his sleeves, already sticking in the overheated, crowded rooms of the Sedgmont's musicale. He looked again at the entrance, trying to be subtle, but Harriet had assured him that Lucy had recovered from her headache and planned to attend tonight's performance. The violinist was supposed to be superb although Aubrey did not believe he would surpass some of the performers he had heard during his stay in Italy.

It still irritated him George had aided Lucy in escaping the park this morning. George insisted that Lucy had not felt well, but then why would he let her ride back alone? What if she became more unwell on the way? No, there was something that George had not told him. He tried to press him in the carriage on their return, but Harriet kept diverting the subject. She talked about the people she had met in the park who might attend the musicale, and so on, and would not answer questions about Lucy.

Not that he felt guilty about his treatment of Lucy. He had only wanted to see if he could arouse jealousy when he had strode off to chat with the insipid Miss Bennett and Lady Amelia North. The old Lucy would not have stood for him abandoning her like that. She would have marched right over and taken his arm, establishing her hold on him. It bothered him that Lucy would rather flee the battle and forsake her rights. Did she no longer care about him? He thought he had made progress during the ride and while helping her down from the tree limb.

She had looked so beautiful with her flushed cheeks, and her curls twined around her face as he lifted her down from that branch. It was all he could do not to kiss her right there, and he had thought she might not be unwilling.

"There she is. Thank goodness." Harriet was nodding her head towards the doorway. He looked up and stiffened, a pain stabbing at his gut.

Lucy stood at the entrance to the room, and she was beautiful. She outshone every other woman in the room. Her dress was an icy blue, covered with little pearls that matched the pearls strung through her chestnut hair. With pale skin, she looked like the queen of winter, remote and disdainful of those who turned to look at her. Her slender arm rested on the sleeve of that black-hearted James Lennox, who should be performing his ducal duties on his estates which in Aubrey's estimation should be far, far away.

Aubrey clenched his fists as Harriet and George moved forward to greet the new arrivals. Lucy was smiling and looking up at Carlisle, that great buffoon, her eyes alight with triumph. She was making a point of ignoring him, but he knew she knew of his presence in the group.

"Carlisle, I did not understand you were back in town." Aversley was genial and welcoming. "I thought you had left for the season."

The tall man almost blushed and looked down at Lucy. "Yes, that had been my intent, but I received a request I could not and would not refuse."

Lucy lowered her eyelashes and put her hand over her mouth as she tittered, then batted her eyelashes at Carlisle. Aubrey couldn't believe his eyes. Lucilla Blount had never flirted a day in her life. She was appallingly bad at it, but the big lout straightened and patted her arm, oblivious to the falsity of her manner.

Aversley looked sideways at his betrothed and Harriet responded with a shrug. "Your Grace, I don't believe you have met our good friend, Viscount Lovell. Lovell, this is His Grace, the Duke of Carlisle."

Carlisle inclined his head, but Lucy pulled his attention away by tugging on his arm.

"Carlisle, I am dreadfully thirsty. Can we get some ratafia? Please?" Lucy crooned at the Duke. Even Carlisle was looking askance at her.

"Of course, my dear, in just a moment. I would like to speak to Lovell here for the nonce."

Lucy's eyes widened, and Harriet rushed forward and took her arm. "Aversley, please get us something to drink while Lady Lucilla and I take a moment in the repairing room? I need her help with something, a flounce." Harriet was flustered, but she sailed off arm-in-arm with Lucy while George gave a short bow and went off to do her bidding.

Carlisle was just a few inches taller than him, and Aubrey hated that. He waited for Carlisle to say whatever he wanted to say, but the man just stood there and looked him up and down. Aubrey risked a peek to see the back of Lucy's head as Harriet dragged her up the stairs to the next floor where the retiring room was situated.

"Have you known Lady Lucilla long?"

Carlisle's voice startled Aubrey and brought his focus back to the man. Apparently, the big buffoon was not as dull as he appeared.

"Her brother's lands run along the boundary of my estate. We have known each other since we were children," Aubrey replied.

"And you have just arrived back from the continent?"

"Yes, I was in Italy for five years." Aubrey was getting irritated at the Duke's inquisition, but there was not much he could do about it at present. There were people all around watching them curiously. Carlisle smirked at him as if the same realization had occurred to him. Then he lost the grin as another thought presented itself.

"Five years? You left England five years ago?" His eyes narrowed as he waited for Aubrey's reply.

Aubrey looked him in the eye. "Yes, Your Grace, I left England five years ago. I was under a misapprehension which caused me to leave, and I am here now to rectify that error."

Carlisle tapped a long elegant finger against his lips while he pondered this admission. "I believe I see." He gave Aubrey a hard stare. "Aversley tells me you are a good man. And if you have a reason for the hurt you did her...," he paused as Aubrey stiffened. "Yes, I can tell it was you. Her unusual manner alone would have given it away. Anyway, I expect that you will redeem yourself and treat her well if she will have you. But if you hurt her, I will hunt you down and see you dead in a most unpleasant manner."

Aubrey gave a low bow, then faced the Duke. "Your Grace, I will never stop trying to make up for the damage I caused Lady Lucilla. I would be the luckiest man on earth if she would have me. And I *do* intend that to be our future — together."

Carlisle winced just a little and Aubrey remembered that the man had asked for Lucy's hand not that long before.

He said in a low voice, "I love her, and I have always loved her. I will not hurt her again."

Carlisle gave a sharp nod. "Please relay my regrets to Lady Lucilla? Another estate emergency has called me away, and I will not be returning soon. I will leave her in your capable hands."

"Thank you, Your Grace. You needn't worry. I will convey your apologies." Carlisle spun around and headed for the door, ignoring the mamas and their daughters trying to gain his attention. Aversley arrived bearing two glasses of ratafia in time to see his back going through the doorway.

"Is Carlisle leaving?" he asked. "I thought he had just arrived. Is he taking Lady Lucilla with him?

"No, I assured him we would bring her home in our carriage. He had an estate emergency."

"Estate emergency? Now?"

Aubrey raised an eyebrow, and George pursed his lips.

"I see."

"See what, my dear?" Harriet and Lucy were back, and Lucy did not look happy. She was turning her head furiously, seeking her errant escort.

"What did you do with Carlisle?" she angrily asked Aubrey. "Where is he?"

Aubrey put his hands up in denial. "I did nothing. He asked me to tell you that another estate emergency has called him away again."

George was bobbing his head. "Yes, yes, Lady Lucilla, and we are to take you home in our carriage after the musicale."

"Which is starting now." Harriet took George's arm and found seats. Aubrey laid Lucy's arm onto his own and followed.

•

Lucy's chest was heaving as she tried to contain her anger, but she was not sure whom to unleash it on. She might suspect that Aubrey was the main culprit, but how could he have got rid of Carlisle? Jamie knew she needed him here tonight. Lucy had been most explicit with him while trying not to tell him too much. She sat next to Harriet and Aubrey took the chair on her other side.

He casually turned to look over his shoulder and his thigh pressed against her leg. Lucy gave a little gasp as heat flared in her belly, but then he turned back leaving his leg touching hers. She tried to inch away, but Harriet frowned at her as the music was about to start. A thin man, Monsieur something or other, stood at the front of the room with a violin. Lucy gave up and waited for the musicale to begin. Somehow Aubrey had acquired a program, and she tried to read what music was being performed this evening. Aubrey did not look up, but he moved the program over and held it up so she could see what it said.

"Hmm, Mozart. I prefer the Baroque period." Lucy sniffed and settled her reticle in her lap.

"I prefer Beethoven. So much more romantic, don't you think?" Aubrey smirked at her and tapped the program. "Ah, but here at the end, he is performing some Paganini. I heard him play when I was in Italy, and he was a virtuoso. We will see if Monsieur LeTours can compare."

Lucy eyed Aubrey curiously, but then the maestro lifted his bow and began to play. The violinist seemed competent to her, and she relaxed, enjoying the Violin Concerto in D Major as the music flowed around them. Almost at once George's head bowed and his eyes closed as he settled in for a nap. Harriet looked and rolled her eyes, but did not wake him. Aubrey, on the other hand, was rapt, engrossed in the performance. But Aubrey was an artist and although not a musician, still sensitive to the creative world. She watched him surreptitiously when he closed his eyes, the better to absorb the music. He was listening and not asleep like poor George. Lucy wondered at the sensitivity of this man who could so appreciate fine arts but ignore the susceptibility of a young girl.

Chapter Eleven

The fresh air outside the Sedgemont's home was welcoming after the heat inside the music room. Lucy, Aubrey, Harriet, and George waited with other attendees for their carriage to arrive at the front of the line. George felt refreshed after his nap and happily expounded on the virtues of violin music for sleeping versus the issues involved with applause at a musicale being a detriment to that same sleeping. Harriet was laughing merrily, not at all embarrassed at her fiancé's faux pas. At least half the men and a few of the older ladies had also recouped some energy from napping.

Aubrey was smiling, but he appeared distracted. He had admitted that the maestro had played the Paganini well, and he had acted the escort for Lucy during the intermission, fetching a drink and then staying by her side.

Lucy did not know what to make of him. He did not seem interested in any of the other young women that thronged the rooms, even as she had pointed out a few of the most eligible ladies, hoping that one of them might attract him. In the depths of her heart, it would have crushed her if he had abandoned her for another, but he had stayed true, never leaving her elbow.

George's carriage arrived, and they all got in. Lucy settled next to Harriet, a little weary. Her stomach had churned all day, waiting to hear from Jamie. Then he had deserted her so fast. Lucy knew she had taken advantage of him, but for him to strand her with Aubrey, well, that was beyond the pale. She could not confide the real reason she needed his escort, so he probably thought she was just frivolous. She could not fault him.

The conversation was desultory on the ride back home. It wasn't until they reached Harriet's home she realized she had a dilemma. Aubrey had perked up and was watching her as Harriet stepped out of the carriage, George handing her down to escort her up her steps. But Lucy had not moved to get out, and in the dim carriage lamps, she could see Aubrey waiting for an explanation. Even if she stepped down from the carriage here, it was too late and too dark for her to walk the three blocks to her brother's townhouse all alone.

George stepped back into the carriage and sat next to Aubrey. He smiled and said, "Since you are both living next door to each other for the time being, there is just one more stop until I can find my pillow." He chuckled and added, "As if I haven't got enough sleep tonight."

Lucy nodded with a small smile, determined not to respond as Aubrey's eyebrows rose higher on his forehead. George was an excellent man, so sweet and perfect for Harriet, but she should have expected this dilemma. If Carlisle had taken her home, she would not have any issues. The events of the evening had discomposed her.

The carriage halted again, and Aubrey got out first so he could hand her down. He could have let the footman perform the task, and she almost said so, but she could see he was waiting for her to say the same. Lucy called goodnight to George from the sidewalk, and the carriage pulled away. She fidgeted with her reticle, trying to pull out the front door key with her gloves on, while Aubrey watched her, arms crossed.

"Problem, sweetheart?" he asked.

"No, and I did not give you permission to call me that." She finally grasped the damn key only to drop it to the sidewalk. Aubrey at once scooped it up from where it had fallen.

"That belongs to me," Lucy said holding out her hand.

"Of course." Aubrey's eyes were twinkling. "Just let me see you to the door." He took Lucy's arm and compelled her to follow him up the stairs. At the door, he ceremoniously placed the key into the lock and turned the handle. "My dear," he said as he bowed her through the entrance.

Before she reacted, he had stepped into the hallway behind her. Mrs. Brundage had left a bracket of candles burning in a sconce on the wall at the foot of the stairs. A single candlestick sat on the table beneath it for Lucy to light her way to her bedroom.

"Where is your butler, your footmen?" Aubrey murmured. Lucy looked down at her feet and mumbled something.

"Lucy, where are your servants?" Aubrey moved a little closer to her, and Lucy busied herself with lighting her candlestick from the sconce and taking it into the parlor behind her. She set the candle on a table and sank down onto a comfortable sofa. Aubrey followed her into the room and sat next to her. She startled and moved further away, but forced herself to stop. She lifted her chin and looked at him.

"I'm staying here with just the housekeeper. She and her husband care for the house when the family is not here. There is no need for more servants when it is just me."

Aubrey wrinkled his brow. "But what about your maid?"

Lucy stood and went over to a cabinet with several bottles. Without asking him, she poured a whiskey for Aubrey and brought it back over to him.

"I don't need a maid most of the time, so I left her in Yorkshire. Mrs. Brundage aids me on the few occasions when I require help with a dress or my hair. Most of what I wear is simple enough to put on or take off..." she trailed off as she saw Aubrey's eyebrows shoot to his hairline. He hastily sipped his whiskey.

Lucy blushed and plucked at her dress. Aubrey put down his glass and put his hand over hers. She stilled, conscious of his hot hand resting on her thigh.

"Lucy, what happened to you? Why are you not married with a cadre of little children hanging onto your skirts?" He watched as she jerked and then drew in a deep breath, but she did not answer him. Instead, a single tear ran down from the corner of her eye. She closed her eyes and tipped her head forward.

"What do you want from me?" Lucy whispered. "Why will you not leave me alone? Why did you come back?" She brought her hands to her face, hiding from him.

"Do not cry, please do not." Aubrey put his arm around Lucy's shoulders, pulling her closer to him. She resisted for a moment and then cuddled into him.

"I am not crying," she sniffed into his chest. "I don't want you to look at me."

Aubrey held her, not sure what to say. She was always so brave, his Lucy, and he had not expected this collapse. But he could not leave her alone. He had always meant her to be his, and he was sure she believed it as well. She was just fighting the reality of their emotions.

She lifted her head, her hands on his chest and her eyes so sad. Aubrey could not help but lean forward and touch his lips to hers, just gentle pressure. She gasped, and like that, she was a searing fire in his arms. Her mouth opened and her tongue invaded his mouth, sweeping against his. She whimpered and tried to move closer, so Aubrey picked her up, never breaking contact with her sweet mouth, and pulled her onto his lap. Aubrey has hard beneath her rump, and he could not help pressing up against her. She was almost frantic, tearing at his cravat, trying to touch his skin.

"Easy sweetheart, we have time," Aubrey crooned at her. She attacked his mouth again as if she did not want him to speak. That was when Aubrey realized that this was wrong, Lucy was too overwrought. He pulled away from her, gently caressing her face, and looked into her eyes. He had always read Lucy's eyes for her feelings, and now he knew.

She was begging him, but she did not know what it was she wanted. Her feelings for him were still too fraught and confused.

Gradually, the passion left her and color rose on her neck. She looked away, embarrassed by her actions. She moved to leave his lap, but Aubrey kept his arm around her waist, holding her in place.

"Let me go please," she said stiffly, not meeting his eyes.

"No, Lucy, I will never let you go. You were always mine, and I am yours."

"I do not even know what you are saying. It was easy enough to leave me before. Why do you bother with me now? Is this a cruel game, to see if you can win me back just to prove your power over me?" She leaped from his arms and hurried across the room.

"Well, you have won. As you see, I succumbed to your wiles again with little effort on your part at all. I am a wanton and now you can leave me." Lucy hissed at him, her shame and bitterness spilling out from deep inside.

Aubrey stood, but did not move towards her, he just studied her where she stood in the dim corner of the room. She had her fist clenched, and her head was up, eyes flashing fire at him. She was magnificent, and he wondered again how he had ever left her, ever believed the lies.

"Lucy, love, it is not a game with me. I want you, and I want you badly. And I want you for always as far as I can see into the future."

She put her hands up, tucking in curls that had come loose, her eyes assessing him. "I see." She walked towards him. "What if I say I will be with you, but only until the wedding?"

"What?" She had shocked him. Aubrey thought frantically, trying to decipher her meaning.

Lucy drew in a breath. "I will be with you in a carnal way, but only until the wedding is over. Then we will part ways and never meet again."

"I want to think about it." Her eyes widened, and she looked unsure. He continued, "I will meet with you tomorrow morning to discuss my terms." Aubrey would not agree until he had looked at every angle of her proposition.

Lucy nodded with a quick shake of her head. "That will do. Then we will meet in the morning."

"Definitely." He lifted her hand and laid a warm kiss on the back. "Until tomorrow."

Chapter Twelve

Lucy had tossed and turned the entire night, unable to stop thinking about her proposal and wondering what Aubrey's answer would be. What did he have to lose? He could spend his next week in her bed at night, and what man in his right mind would decline the chance to bed a woman, any woman? Admittedly, she did not have that much experience with men, but she did not think most males would refuse her scheme if a woman offered the same to them.

She could feel her cheeks heat thinking of the brazen manner she had propositioned him. But trying to ignore him had not worked. Perhaps he would decide that she was no longer worth pursuing. He had been distant last evening though she had not expected that he would throw her down on the floor and ravish her. Lucy had not forgiven Aubrey for leaving her, but maybe she could purge him from her thoughts if they spent their nights together for the next week. Perhaps this was the best way to get him out of her system.

Seeing him again after five years had stirred up many feelings she thought suppressed from her life, visions that now only appeared in the occasional dream. She had made her peace, she thought, and her life was comfortable as it was. She never expected to marry, and she had a fulfilling life and a daily routine in Yorkshire. If she had occasionally yearned for something different, it was of no matter.

She finished dressing and wandered down the stairs to the kitchen. Since it was just her and Mr. and Mrs. Brundage in the house, she had fallen into the habit of taking her breakfast in the kitchen at the open table. There was no sense in making the housekeeper prepare a tray for her or set up the dining room. Lucy was comfortable with the Brundages whom she had known since she was a child.

Mrs. Brundage was busy kneading bread at the table. When Richard and his wife were in residence, there were many more servants and a cook to prepare their meals. But the housekeeper could quite provide nourishing and flavorful meals for Lucy.

"Good morning!" Lucy said brightly.

"And a good morning to you, my lady." The rosy-cheeked woman smiled at Lucy. "What would you like to eat this day? Anything special? I have kippers left from Mr. Brundage's meal."

"Thank you, no to the kippers. I think I would just like fruit and a cup of chocolate. My stomach is a little unsettled this morning, and I did not sleep well so I would like something light to eat."

"Right away, my lady. Would you rather have tea? I can make up a cup that would calm your insides." Mrs. Brundage was practically clucking at Lucy.

"No, the chocolate will be perfect. I rarely indulge in a sweet treat, and I am enjoying it while I can do so here."

Mrs. Brundage looked at her oddly, and Lucy realized that chocolate was available at her brother Richard's table every morning and the housekeeper likely knew it. She bit her lip, hoping that the woman would not inquire further. She already suspected her because Lucy had not brought her maid or any other servants. Richard had sent her in his coach so Mrs. Brundage accepted that the Earl knew of her visit, but in the housekeeper's experience young ladies did not travel without their maids. Unless she went out with Harriet, Lucy stayed in the house as she did not want to offend the woman any further.

"I think I will just take a tray out into the garden. It is such a beautiful day." Lucy decided it would be better to be away from Mrs. Brundage's scrutiny.

The housekeeper gave her a shrewd glance, but nodded and prepared the tray. She held open the door while Lucy passed out into the back where there was a small garden. Her sister-in-law Anne often broke her fast out there when in town or they had their tea at the little table set out there in the shade.

She set the tray down and sat down with a sigh. Aubrey had said he would decide today, but she did not know when she would see him - unless he meant the ball they were both supposed to attend tonight? Lucy was not sure at this point whether she wanted him to say yes or to refuse her. She wanted to believe if he said yes, then they would both be ready to move on after the wedding. But there was a small niggle of doubt that while he might be prepared to leave her quickly enough, the experience might leave her devastated again. At least, she would be ready this time. She picked up her chocolate and took a sip.

AUBREY PUT DOWN HIS brush and stepped back, studying the portrait on his easel critically. He still did not have the look in her eyes correctly. But her lips curved into a smile that Aubrey hoped to see her reflect later that day. Her proposition had surprised, even shocked him, but there was not a chance in the world he would refuse her. Aubrey had asked for time only to ensure that Lucy knew her own mind. If she insisted on using the wedding as a deadline, he would agree all the while knowing he would never fulfill that pledge. Lucy was his forever even if she did not yet acknowledge it. Aubrey knew there would never be another woman for him.

He walked over to the window. Aubrey had slept soundly and arisen early this morning, eager to work on his painting. He glanced to the left to the backyard of the adjoining house. Richard, Earl of Wakefield, seldom came to town, much like his father before him. His townhouse was half the size of Aubrey's home since the family rarely used it, only when the House of Lords was in session. While Aubrey had a sizable garden in the back of his house, Wakefield had a tiny plot of land. Lady Lovell's gardeners kept Aubrey's garden in rigorous control, sterile in precise rows of plants and nary a flower to be found. Wakefield's oasis rioted in bright colors and green leaves that straggled across the yard and should have overwhelmed the tiny plot but instead gave it a life that never crossed the wall between the houses.

There was a movement next door, and he saw Lucy sitting out in the sunlight sipping a cup of something, tea maybe. He smiled, watching her stare out at her garden, knowing she was unaware of his presence. Aubrey turned and threw a cloth over the easel and pulled off the smock he used to protect his clothes, then passed out of the room. He went down the stairs and through the hallway to the sunny conservatory off the back corner of the house. There were a door and path there that lead to the back gate. From there he could step down the lane to the gateway into Wakefield's backyard.

The door was unlocked, and Aubrey walked into the yard and over to where Lucy sat at a small table. She looked up, startled, as the gate opened and he saw her tense as she recognized him. She put both her hands on her lap and waited for him to seat himself.

Aubrey did not intend to tease Lucy, but he was glad to see that his decision mattered to her. She would not be so edgy if she did not care, and that gave him hope he was on the right path.

"Good morning, Lucy," he said. "Such a lovely day, don't you think?"

Lucy blinked, but replied with a slight edge, "Yes, lovely."

"And how did you sleep last night?"

"That is a somewhat personal question to ask a lady!" Yes, she was irritated, Aubrey thought. She did not look as if she had slept well last night.

"Excuse me, my lady, but if I concede to your request, then I think personal questions might become de rigueur."

Two spots of red appeared on Lucy's cheeks, and her eyes narrowed. Aubrey liked to see Lucy unsettled, but he thought it might be time for a strategic retreat.

"But never mind all that. I have thought a lot about your proposal, and I agree but with some conditions of my own."

"What conditions?" Lucy asked quickly.

"If we decide to continue our liaison after the wedding, then that decision will suspend your condition about one week for the duration of our dalliance."

"That won't happen. I will return home after Harriet's wedding."

"Perhaps I will charm you into staying in London. Or if I return to Lovell Moor, then we will be in proximity." Aubrey had no intention of continuing their arrangement as a liaison but as a much more permanent arrangement. Still, he wanted to test her resolve.

"We will not meet in Yorkshire, Lord Lovell. That is one thing I am sure of." Lucy was emphatic.

"Perhaps. But I believe we should leave that option open. Do you not agree?"

"I care not. For my part, our relationship ends on the day of Harriet and George's wedding. You can believe anything you wish." Lucy was reacting to his teasing much as the young girl she had once been and Aubrey suppressed a grin.

"Then I agree with your proposition," he said and bit the inside of his cheek to keep from laughing as Lucy's mouth gaped.

"What?"

"I am honored to accept your proposal, Lady Lucilla. Now that that's out of the way I have something I would like to show you."

"Now?"

Aubrey could see Lucy's mind-boggling right before his eyes as her thoughts misinterpreted his current intentions. His own hopes were in alignment with her views, but he could wait until the evening to consummate their agreement. He had no intention of ruining her reputation.

"Yes, would you come with me next door? I would like your opinions on some of my paintings. I have always found your observations to be of value, and I have no one else to show them to."

Lucy took a deep breath, eying him suspiciously. "I am delighted to opine on your art. I'm so glad you are still painting."

"That was pretty much all I did during my time in Italy." He stood and held out his arm to escort her to his home. "Come."

Chapter Thirteen

Lucy laid her arm on top of Aubrey's and allowed him to escort her to the back gate, down the lane, and into his yard. She thought about Mrs. Brundage watching her leave unchaperoned with a strange man, but she decided that she could deal with that later when she returned. As far as the housekeeper knew, Aubrey St. Clare was just a neighbor, an acquaintance from Lucy's youth.

Aubrey led her from the conservatory out into a hallway where a startled footman hastily turned away when he saw his master enter with an unknown female. Lucy pulled on his arm a little, but he continued on up the stairs to the second floor where he had situated his studio. Lucy's eyes widened as they walked past several bedrooms including the master, but Aubrey did not stop. She relaxed as he opened the door to his studio and she could see that the room was plainly used for his painting.

He walked over to where he had several canvases stacked against a wall and turned them, so they faced her in a line down an empty section of wall. They were all scenes of Italy, countryside with tall green trees laden with yellow lemons, cityscapes of small crooked houses painted in pastel colors, and seascapes with small sailboats showing brightly colored sails. Aubrey stepped back as Lucy came forward and bent to study the painting at the end. She crept down the line, standing and stopping at each scene.

Aubrey watched her, admiring her grace and her form as she studied his work. He was nervous that she might not like the pictures, but his joy at having her here in his home overtook that feeling. Just two weeks before Aubrey thought he might never see her again and now she was here and would be his forever if he had anything to say about it. He was sure he could persuade her. They had been so in love during their youth. He had never fallen out of love with her, and he knew she felt the same about him. She was just having more difficulty coming to realize it. Aubrey knew Lucy had agreed to bed him because she thought would get him out of her heart and mind. He intended that her scheme fail and she become more entangled with him instead.

He purposely stepped next to her, subtly inhaling the scent of lavender emanating from her hair. She did not look at him as she asked, "Are these paintings of Italy from the area where you were living?"

"Yes, they are from La Spezia and the Ligurian region where I lived for the last five years."

Lucy nodded, still examining the pictures. "They are lovely, Aubrey. You have grown as an artist. These are worthy of an exhibition at the Royal Academy."

"Thank you, Lucy." He swallowed hard, forcing the words from his throat. Aubrey could not find any other words. Lucy had always been honest, and she had an innate gift for color and detail in her criticisms. If she liked the paintings, then it was enough to satisfy him.

"There are no people in them. You used to do portraits."

"The only person I have ever painted is you."

She turned to him, her eyes wide in surprise. "Surely that is not so."

"I am afraid that it is true." He let out a self-deprecating puff of sound and shrugged. "You are my muse, Lucy. That has always been the truth. It still is and always will be true."

Aubrey reached for her hand and pulled her across the room to where another stack of canvases laid facing against the wall. He took the first one and turned it around so that Lucy could see the portrait of herself sitting on her horse, her hair flying loose as she turned to look at something off to the side. The next canvas showed Lucy sitting on a wall, her arms full of wildflowers. A smaller canvas showed a sleeping

Lucy lying on a blanket under one of the elm trees that bordered a meadow where she and Aubrey had often gone to picnic. Picture after picture showed Lucy in different poses, smiling or with thoughtful gazes looking out from the various portraits. The last one showed Lucy nude on a blanket, one hand shyly covering her nether curls while the other hand curled around her head. Her hair was down, just barely covering one pink-tipped breast.

She drew in a deep breathe. "I did not pose for any of these," she said.

"I know. They were all done from memory while I was in Italy."

"You were thinking of me?" Aubrey could see the uncertainty in her eyes, the flash of doubt, and he pulled her to him.

"Every minute," he said and crushed his lips to hers. Lucy moaned, and he pulled her closer until he could feel her breasts heaving against his chest. He thrust his tongue into her mouth, and she responded with her own, swirling and mating with his.

Aubrey pivoted, pulling Lucy around and against the wall. Her hands were around his neck and pulling on his hair, trying to join his mouth back to hers, but he did not care. Aubrey nipped down the side of her neck, nibbling tenderly where her pulse beat at the base of her throat. He pulled the fichu out of the collar of her dress and hooked a finger inside the bodice, trying to pull it down while he rained kisses on her chest. There was a rip, and Lucy gasped, but Aubrey would not stop now. She was moaning in a constant low undertone; his Lucy had always been vocal in her lovemaking.

They both froze when there was a knock at the door. Aubrey turned his head to stare as if he could see through the wood and force whoever was there away.

"My lord," a voice called.

He closed his eyes and tried to gain control of his errant body, stepping away from Lucy. She gasped and pulled at the torn remnants of her dress. Lucy searched the ground frantically for her fichu and dove for it as if the thin piece could still cover the bare expanse of her chest.

Aubrey sighed and called out, "Yes, what is it?"

The voice, one of his footmen, John, he thought, replied. "Baron Aversley is downstairs to see you, my lord. He said you had an appointment to go out."

Aubrey closed his eyes and shook his head. "Fine, yes, I will be there in a moment. Please let him know I am delayed for a short time." He reached down to adjust himself, then studied Lucy's attempt at making herself presentable.

"Here," he grabbed the smock he used to cover his clothes when painting. "Try this. I'm sorry, both that I ripped your dress and that I let this get out of hand. I forgot that I had a meeting with George this morning. He wants my advice on a bridal gift for Harriet before we all leave for his estate for the wedding week."

Lucy had her eyes cast down as she wrapped herself in the garment. "It is fine. I should never have come up here alone with you."

Aubrey reached out and clasped her lightly by the upper arms. "Lucy, it is my fault. I wanted you to see my paintings." He grinned. "And I intended to wait until tonight when we are in your bed to.."

Lucy interrupted him, her face bright red. "No, please, I do not know. Perhaps we should not..."

"Yes, we should." Aubrey cut her off, shaking her slightly to emphasize his words. He did not want her to have any doubts at this stage, and he emphasized his seriousness. "You agreed, Lucy. You were the initiator, not that it took any great urging on my part. You and I are meant to be together, and this is just the first step. Again, I apologize for my previous actions, but I have been thinking about us together for a very, very long time." He smiled at her. "But I believe I can wait for a few more hours."

Lucy bit her lip and then nodded her head. "Is that what you intend, to come to my bed?"

"If it is agreeable to you, I think it would be best. You have fewer servants to worry about than I. I will escort you home from the Mautravers' ball this evening and slip inside with you as long as no one is about. And speaking of that, I will see you home now before we raise George's suspicions. I can take you back the way we came in."

"But your servants," Lucy twisted the fichu in her hands, having given up on replacing it in her torn bodice.

"They are discreet. It will be fine, Lucilla." He caressed her cheek softly. He did not think they would gossip, but only no one would care once she was his wife. "Come, we should go."

Chapter Fourteen

The Mautravers' ball was a crush. George led Harriet into the ballroom, but someone they knew stopped them every few moments. Aubrey kept Lucy by his side, never pausing until they reached a clear spot on the far side of the huge room. He nodded at a few of his friends but ignored the young ladies who tried to attract his attention and their overeager mamas. Lucy meekly walked beside him. She had been quiet ever since they had picked her and Harriet up in the carriage. The two of them had got ready for the ball at Harriet's home, and he had had no chance to speak to her privately. But Aubrey intended to find out what the matter was. He did not want her to have doubts or second thoughts now.

He looked over at her, but she was watching the dancers, a small frown on her lips. There were faint dark circles under her eyes, testifying to her lack of sleep the night before.

"Lady Lucilla, how are you this evening?"

She looked startled at his formal address but attempted a smile. "I am fine, my lord. And how are you? I hope you had a good day as the weather was so beautiful."

"Weather, Lucy?" He leaned in and whispered as no one was around that at the moment. "Really? You want to talk about the weather?"

A mulish look came over her face, and her eyes flashed fire at him. Better, he thought.

"And what subject would you wish to converse about, Lord Lovell?" There was an edge to her tone, but Aubrey ignored it. Her hand was still on his arm, and it trembled. He covered it with his own and gave it a squeeze, then released it as he realized there were hundreds of eyes around them.

"Lucy," he said in a low tone. "Would you rather forego our assignation this evening?"

She tensed, then looked out over the crowd. "Why, do you have a better offer for tonight?" She held her chin high, and her eyes were distant.

Aubrey felt his guts roil. He would not force her if she were genuinely having doubts. But he needed to be with her, needed to show her all the love he could not express with the crowds that always seemed to be around them. Lucy would not believe him unless he could show her. Words would not sway her after the way Aubrey had abandoned her before. It must be just nerves. Gad, he was nervous himself, had worried all day about the various ways that things could go wrong.

Lucy glanced sideways at him, waiting for him to respond. Spots of color appeared on her cheekbones, and she bit her lip.

"Of course not," he said, trying not to show his frustration. "I was just thinking of you in case..."

"Lovell, my dear, I was not sure you planned to attend this evening."

Aubrey stiffened as his mother came up to them. She gave Lucy a hard glance but then ignored her as she leaned forward to kiss his cheek. His eyes narrowed in suspicion wondering what she was up to. His mother was not affectionate and most certainly not after their last discussion.

"Mother, I did not expect to see you tonight, or any night for that matter. I thought you were staying at your sister's home."

Lucy pulled her hand away from his arm, and Aubrey wanted to snatch it back, but could not with his mother standing there. There would be a scene, he could tell.

"Oh, it was boring there, and I had already accepted several engagements in town I did not want to miss."

"Mother, you remember Lady Lucilla Blount." Aubrey watched Lucy give a small curtsy to the older woman, and the Dowager Lady Lovell gave a brief nod of acknowledgment.

"Lady Lucilla, how are your brother and dearest Anne. You must be eager to return home as Lady Wakefield nears her term, I should think." Lady Lovell reached out and patted Lucy's shoulder.

"They are well, I thank you. And yes, I am anxious to return to Yorkshire."

"Dreadful place, so far away. I prefer town much more. But you will excuse me please and let me borrow my son for a moment. The Duke of Clairmont would like to speak to him. He has not had the opportunity since Lovell returned home."

"I believe I see my friend Lady Harriet waving over there." Aubrey looked, but Harriet was merrily dancing with George, her back to Lucy. Before he could say anything, Lucy had given another small curtsy and hied off to the other side of the room. Aubrey turned to his mother, but she took his arm, ready for him to escort her to the corner where the Duke of Clairmont stood with a small crowd around him. Aubrey sighed and led her across the floor, but he tracked Lucy's dark hair as she walked to the edge of the room.

———

LUCY FOUND A CORNER where she could stop and collect herself. She turned to the wall as if studying the plant placed there and put her hands on her hot cheeks and closed her eyes. This was not going to work. She should just go back to Yorkshire now, tonight. She did not know what she had been thinking to make that proposal to Aubrey and then today in Aubrey's house she had utterly lost her wits. How shameless she was. And he did not even appear to care one way or the other. She suspected if she did just disappear, he would rapidly find another mistress among the widows and light-skirts in town. He had only agreed to her because he found it convenient.

She gathered herself and turned back to the room. Lucy scanned the dancers until she found Harriet and George going through the steps of a country dance. She would tell Harriet that she must return home at once, an emergency she could not put off.

Lucy drew in a breath as she saw Aubrey standing across the room with his mother and the Duke of Clairmont. A petite blonde girl was laughing up at him, and he smiled down at her, apparently amused by her prattle. The girl was beautiful. The Duchess of Clairmont approached and took her husband's arm, and Lucy realized that the girl must be their daughter. She had the look of her mother who had been a diamond of the highest water in her time. Lady Lovell was beaming, and Lucy realized that the parents were setting up a match between the younger people.

Her heart hurt, and she brought a hand up to cover where it lay beneath her skin as if that might protect it. It should not matter to her. Aubrey needed to marry someone and beget heirs. Why not the daughter of a Duke?

His intentions towards her were clear and again, why not? She had propositioned him after all so he would take what she would give and then leave once more. What had she been thinking? How foolish of her to believe she could ever cleave Aubrey St Clare from her heart.

Lucy felt tears starting and blinked, not wanting to make a scene. She saw doors leading out to the back gardens. It was not wise for her to go out there alone, but perhaps it would be all right if she stayed near the door.

A waltz started, and she saw Aubrey bow to the blonde girl and lead her out to dance. She spun on her heel and headed for the doorway.

The night air was much cooler than the stuffy ballroom. She put her gloved hands to her eyes, pressing against them to stop her tears. It would not do for her to give into despair once more.

"What is this? Has your cavalier deserted you?" Lucy stiffened and lowered her hands. Rathburn stood in front of her, his handsome face disfigured by a smirk as he crowed at her distress.

"I stepped outside for some fresh air. Please leave me alone."

"I think not. It would not do for me as a gentleman to leave such a sad lady alone. Why, any rogue might accost you."

"You mean a rogue like you," Lucy said rudely. She did not care about offending Rathburn; she wanted him to go away.

He chuckled, amused by her boldness. He had been watching her since she came into the ballroom, waiting for his chance. Rathburn had seen Lady Lovell approach her son and spirit him away. It would seem that she did not approve of the relationship between her son and Lady Lucilla Blount. That was an interesting thought he tucked away for consideration at a future time.

"Lucy, Lucy, that is not the way a lady reacts to an offer of gallantry," he cooed.

"I did not give you leave to use my name, my lord. And if you will not go away, then I must." She tried to pass by him, but he reached out and took her arm, holding her in place. She looked over his shoulder at the doorway to the ballroom. It would not do for anyone to see her here with him. The scandal last time had been tremendous, and another one now would ruin Harriet's wedding.

Lucy gritted her teeth. "Let go of me."

"I think not." He tapped his chin with one slender finger, contemplating the woman in front of him. She was a rich prize even with her soiled reputation. "Lovell is not missing you, so who else will look for you? And you do not wish to create a fuss, do you? No, I think perhaps we might stroll further down into the gardens." He gripped her arm tighter as she tried to pull away.

Lucy drew in a deep breath and stilled. Then she lifted her leg in the manner her brother, Richard, had shown her. Her knee connected with the juncture of Rathburn's thighs, right where a man was most susceptible. His eyes widened, and he released her as he cupped himself where she had injured him.

Lucy hurriedly passed by him and reentered the ballroom. She kept her head down and skirted around the room to the entry. Almost running, she left, only stopping to leave a message for Harriet with one of the wigged footmen in the foyer.

"I am not feeling well and must leave. I am taking the carriage, but I will send it back for Baron Aversley and his party. Please tell Lady Harriet Everton from Lady Lucilla Blount." She moved out into the fresh night air and found the carriage waiting down the street.

Chapter Fifteen

Aubrey was in a foul mood. It was bad enough that his mother had been at the ball last evening, transparently trying to match make. He felt he could not be rude to the Duke of Clairmont and had agreed to her less than subtle machinations. He had even danced with Lady Clarissa, the Duke's daughter. She was a pretty young thing, a typical English rose, and it was not her fault they had trapped him into a dance with her. And she had conversed easily with him during their waltz, unlike many young ladies out for their first season. He was sure she was quite the catch on the marriage mart.

He kept searching for Lucy as he twirled around the room. She had disappeared, at least, he could not find her. Harriet and George danced by, Harriet giving him a frown when she saw him dancing with Lady Clarissa. When the dance ended, he had handed her back to her parents with a bow and shrugged off his mother trying to keep him in their circle. Aubrey stalked the ballroom and had walked out onto the terrace where a few couples strolled back and forth in the light reflected from inside. Not finding Lucy there, he had strode back into the ballroom to look for Harriet and George.

They were standing to one side, Thornton and Blakesley talking with them. But Lucy was not with them. He scanned the room again, hoping to find her among the dancers, but he could not see her dark hair anywhere.

"Have you seen Lady Lucilla?" he asked the others, breaking into their conversation.

"Lose her, did you?" Aubrey was in no mood for Blakesley's humor, and he gave him an impatient look.

Harriet's eyebrows went up, and she glanced at George, who shrugged. "Lady Lucilla went home. She was not feeling well. I thought you must know already."

Aubrey felt his neck grow hot. Surely Lucy knew he could not help the dance with Lady Clarissa. It meant nothing; he was just appeasing his mother. Then Aubrey smiled to himself. Perhaps she was jealous. Lucy should know she had no reason to be, she was the only woman for him, but maybe this was a good thing. Or a bad thing if it gave her an excuse to not be with him. He could not decide.

He noticed the four sets of eyes on him. Harriet was distinctly disturbed, George looked sheepish, Blakesley was still amused, and Thornton looked thoughtful.

"No, she did not tell me she felt ill. I would have escorted her home if I had known."

The conversation moved to other subjects, and Aubrey impatiently awaited the time when he could take his leave. Finally, he could not bear to linger any further and took his leave of his friends. He hailed a hackney and made his way home. Lucy's house was dark. He walked up the steps to try the door, sure she would have left it unlocked for him, but it would not budge. Aubrey knocked lightly, hoping she would open it for him, but there was no response. He stepped back and looked up at the house as if he might find a magic way inside, but every window was closed tight. He walked around to the side, hoping that the servant door might provide access, but he was foiled again.

Aubrey had his answer. Lucy was angry, and now he had to make amends quickly. He trudged to his home and let himself in. A sleepy footman was waiting, and Aubrey nodded as he ascended the stairs to his bedroom. He undressed as he had not acquired a valet since his return. Aubrey had dressed himself for the last five years, so it did not seem to be a critical need. He dropped into the bed, brain racing, wondering what to do with Lucy. This was not the evening he had planned for them.

IN THE MORNING, THINGS did not improve. Today was the day he and George were leaving with the ladies for George's estate in Kent where the wedding would take place. They would be there for a few days, time he had hoped to spend with Lucy. The other guests would arrive later for the house party that would culminate in the wedding ball and ceremony. Harriet and Lucy rode inside the carriage with Harriet's maid while he and George rode outside. Lucy had been pale and composed, polite but withdrawn. Harriet had given him a worried look, and he hoped that she would plead his case on the ride to the estate.

The weather was pleasant, and George rambled on, talking about estate matters and the wedding plans. Aubrey answered when necessary, but brooded as he watched the coach travel along the road. It only took a few hours to reach George's estate, an elegant Georgian manor of red brick with black shutters. The park was not spacious, but the estate was well laid out.

Harriet and Lucy stepped down from the carriage and entered the house while he and George were dismounting and handing their horses over to the grooms. By the time they entered the building, Lucy was already ascending the stairs following a maid while Harriet waited in the hallway wringing her hands.

"Lucy plans to lie down before dinner as she has a headache from the coach ride."

Aubrey watched as Lucy disappeared from his sight and sighed. "Were you able to speak to her during the ride at all?"

"No, she kept her eyes closed and rested due to a headache, she said. I'm sorry Aubrey, but she does not seem angry, just tired perhaps."

He nodded. "Thank you." He changed subjects, wanting to think about this later when he was alone. "George, do you have plans now for me? I am here to serve you this week, you know."

George laughed. "Let me show you to your room. I intend to get myself cleaned up after our ride, and I suggest you do the same. Nothing is pressing at this point. My lady has everything in hand."

Harriet smiled. "I'm glad you think so, but I agree that we should retire to our rooms and our toilettes. We can meet again before dinner." She took George's arm, and they ascended the stairs.

Aubrey followed, wondering if Harriet would discreetly show which room Lucy was in when they reached the upper hallway. The house was not overly large but could accommodate the wedding guests, at least, those coming for the house party. Many others would stay in neighboring houses or inns just for the night of the ball and the wedding breakfast. But he was not in her good graces enough she would give him an inkling of where they had put Lucy. He did not think George would cross her either. The Dowager Lady Aversley was arriving soon to chaperone and to oversee the festivities, at least as much as George was allowing her to do so. Lady Aversley and Harriet maintained a cordial facade with each other, but the next few days might be tense unless the ladies reached a compromise over the wedding activities.

When the dinner gong sounded, Aubrey was already waiting in the drawing room. George's mother and sister were already seated there as well as George and Harriet. But Lucy had not appeared as yet.

"Is Lady Lucilla planning to attend dinner?" he asked when there was a pause in the conversation.

"No, she took a tray in her room this evening. I expect that she will feel better in the morning."

"Young ladies today suffer too much from weak constitutions," Lady Aversley contributed her part to the conversation. Her daughter Charlotte rolled her eyes behind her, but George took his mother's arm to lead her into the dining room before anyone had time to disagree with the matriarch.

"Yes, yes, mama. Shall we eat now?" He nodded behind her head to Aubrey, who took both Charlotte and Harriet by the arm.

Breakfast the next morning was no better. Lucy did not appear, and then Aubrey left to ride the estate with George. He was feeling quite desperate, and he did not like it. How was he going to win Lucy over if he could not meet with her, talk to her and cajole her?

They stopped in the nearby village for lunch, and Aubrey almost confided in George. But the man was so ecstatic about his upcoming nuptials that Aubrey did not want to say or do anything that might burst his bubble.

Aubrey's luck changed when they returned in the afternoon. The ladies were in the drawing-room, Harriet and Charlotte chattering away and making plans while Lady Aversley looked on in silence. A truce between mother and future daughter-in-law appeared to have been drawn for the week. Lucy was also there with a paper and quill, recording lists as the ladies spoke, crossing lines out again as one or the other decided not to pursue an idea. She looked up, her face solemn, as the men walked into the room still dusty from their ride.

While George greeted the others, Aubrey crossed to Lucy.

"I am glad to see you have recovered. I hope you are feeling much better today."

She gave him a small smile. "Yes, thank you, much better. And how was your ride? This is a pleasant area, is it not?"

He searched her face, but it was inscrutable. She was dealing in pleasantries while he wanted to whisk her away and kiss her until she yielded with a real response.

Harriet called to her, and she turned away to respond. Aubrey clenched his fists in frustration, but stood, hoping for an opportunity for further speech.

"And what are you ladies up to this afternoon?" George was full of bonhomie, pleased that his mother had given up and made peace with his intended.

Harriet responded, "I would like a walk in the gardens. We have been cooped up in here with our tasks, and it is such a pleasant day. I believe all is in order, so we are due for some leisure."

"Let us clean the dust from the road off of ourselves and then we will be at your service." George nodded at Aubrey, who hesitated, not wanting to lose any chance with Lucy, but she seemed to concede to the proposed activity, so he followed him to change his jacket and wash up.

The group of young people met in the hallway, Lady Aversley having retired to her room for a rest. George escorted Harriet and Charlotte, who were now the best of friends, so Aubrey offered his arm to Lucy. She took it readily enough, and they followed the others outside.

George's gardens were not expansive, but some paths led into a lovely wooded area and around a small pond. When some distance had opened between them and the group ahead of them, Aubrey decided that now was the time to speak.

"Lucy, are you unhappy with me? Have I offended you?"

She took a breath and gave him a small smile. "I am sorry if I have given you that impression. I did not mean to. Perhaps you should write it off to a woman's vagaries."

He studied her face, but it remained placid, not a hint of any inner turmoil. She suffered his scrutiny and then tugged at his arm. "We should catch up with the others."

Chapter Sixteen

Lucy got ready for bed and was standing by the window waiting for Aubrey. He had said nothing specific, but she knew he was coming to her tonight. Aubrey had walked her up the stairs to her room when everyone was retiring, and he knew her bedroom was down three doors from his. Aubrey was coming to her tonight.

He had been solicitous all during dinner and after when they had withdrawn to the sitting room. They had played cards, and he had made his intentions known by light touches and knowing looks. She supposed that if she chose, Lucy could turn the lock and keep him out, but she had decided last night as she tossed and turned in her bed.

She loved him, had always loved him, and would love him for the rest of her life. Lucy had made her peace with that decision late the night before. She had felt so many emotions in the last few days: anger, jealousy, despair, and finally acceptance. And if he wanted her, even for a short time, Lucy would acquiesce, at least until the wedding was over and her deadline was met. Then Lucy would return home where she would have her memories to hold her for the rest of her life.

She realized Aubrey was trying to make reparations for abandoning her five years earlier. They had left their relationship in limbo, and he needed to bring it to a satisfactory conclusion for his own peace of mind. Then he could move on with his life, find a woman, Lady Clarissa or whoever he chose, to marry and start a family with. And Lucy would continue with her own life.

The door opened behind her, but Lucy stayed where she was. It was a warm night, and she had opened the window to let in the breeze. It wafted past her and lifted a curl across her breast, then ruffled the lace on her nightgown.

Aubrey moved across the room and stood behind her, not touching, but she could feel the heat of his body. He placed his hands on her waist and drew her back against him. The smell of Aubrey, once so familiar, surrounded her, and she sighed and lifted a hand up to caress his neck as he leaned his head forward against her curls.

"Lucy," he breathed into her ear. She smiled and waited.

"Oh, Lucy." Aubrey pulled her tighter against him. She could feel him hard against her buttocks, and a shiver ran down her spine. Lucy turned in his arms and reached up to pull his head down to her. His lips came down hard on hers, and she reveled in their touch. She felt a moan break free from the pit of her stomach and her mouth opened, tongue intertwining with his. Aubrey placed his hands on either side of her face, holding her firmly in his grasp while he drew in her sweetness. He tasted faintly of tooth powder and Lucy bit at his lower lip, then soothed the spot with her tongue.

Aubrey reached down and gathered the material of her nightgown, pulling it up and over her head. Her arm caught in one sleeve and he helped her to free it, his eyes dark in the dim candlelight of the bedroom. Lucy's nightgown drifted to the floor, and she stepped away, intent on reaching the bed. Aubrey reached out and stopped her.

"Wait. I want to look at you. I want to remember this moment, and I will paint it, so we have it forever."

Lucy blushed but stood obediently as Aubrey gazed at her from the tip of her toes to the top of her disheveled hair.

"You are so beautiful." He dropped his robe and now it was Lucy's turn to look her full. He was naked, and she thought back to when she had last seen him thus. They had both been younger, and though she still looked good, her figure had aged from a girl to a woman with fuller breasts and hips. Likewise, he was broader across the chest, and his skin was darker, showing he had stayed out in the sun without a shirt during his time in Italy.

He scooped her up, and she laughed as he carried her to the bed.

"I believe this is the first time we have used a bed." It was true. Five years ago their lovemaking had taken place out-of-doors on a blanket where they had been picnicking. They had made love twice after Aubrey had proposed marriage, the first time carefully and awkwardly, the next time eagerly, secure in their feelings for the other. Then he was gone the next day, but Lucy pushed that thought out of her mind. He was here - for now.

Aubrey lay down next to her and gathered her to him. He kissed her again, their bodies pressed against each other. Aubrey pushed closer, insinuating a leg between hers and she hooked her top leg over his hip. That put him where she needed him, well, almost where she needed him.

He was kissing his way down her neck now, a small nip where her pulse was beating hard at the base of her neck. Lucy ran her hand through his hair, tugging to bring him back to her mouth.

He lifted his head and chuckled. "My love, I thought I would never hear those sweet sounds coming from your lips again."

Lucy pushed at his chest, embarrassed at his teasing. His face turned serious, and he bent to touch his lips gently to hers. She sighed and kissed him back. He pushed her curls back where they strayed across one cheek and cupped her face, balancing on his elbows. His eyes were gentle with a look she recognized from years before, but no longer believed.

"I need you," she whispered. "Please." And he obliged.

When their breathing slowed and Aubrey rolled over on one side, but he turned Lucy so that her back cuddled into his chest and held her tight against him. He buried his nose into her neck, burrowing through the wild chestnut curls.

"Are you all right?" he asked.

"I'm fine," she answered sleepily. "What about you?"
"All is finally right in my world."
Lucy nodded as she drifted off to sleep.

Chapter Seventeen

When Lucy woke, Aubrey was gone. They had made love twice more during the night, and she was slow to awaken. She had vaguely known he had left her earlier, kissing her goodbye when he went back to his own room before the servants were up.

Lucy stretched, and a twinge of soreness reminded her of the night's activities. She smiled, not minding the aches at all. The last night had been the happiest of her life and Lucy would not regret a minute of it. If anything, the slight twinges reminded her of her joy at the night past. She refused to think of the future and would live for what she could get in these next few days.

She bounded out of bed and washed and dressed in a hurry. Lucy hoped that she could catch Aubrey at breakfast, not for any particular reason except that she wanted to see him. Lucy felt like the seventeen-year-old girl she had once been.

She entered the breakfast room in a rush, stopping to greet Harriet and Charlotte. Lady Aversley took her breakfast on a tray in her room, but Lucy expected to see the men at the table. She felt her stomach drop just a little at their absence, and some of her happiness leeched away. She fixed herself a plate from the buffet and sat next to Harriet. Once Harriet spoke, her joy disappeared altogether.

"Good morning. I trust you slept well." Lucy nodded, her mouth full of coddled eggs, her busy night contributing to her hunger this morning. "The house party guests arrive today, so I hope you are ready for your new roommate.

She swallowed and frowned, confused by what Harriet had said.

Harriet laughed. "I knew you would forget. What with all the people coming I am to share your room until the wedding." She blushed, thinking about whose room she would share after the wedding and Charlotte giggled. Harriet sent her a reproving look and continued, "Everyone will need to share rooms mostly. I have put Blakesley in with Lovell. Charlotte will share with Aunt Lavinia." Charlotte pouted, not pleased with that arrangement. "Just think, Lucy, it will be so much fun, the two of us trading secrets and gossip."

Lucy forced a smile. "I had forgotten, but it will be nice to be together for this while."

"This way Blake can do for both of us." Blake was Harriet's maid. Lucy was used to doing without a maid, but she nodded and took another bite of eggs, her mind racing. Sharing bedrooms would make it impossible for her to be with Aubrey again. She had thought she would have until the wedding to be with him, but that hope had disappeared with Harriet's words. There would be no more nights making love in her bed.

"Where are the men off to this morning?" Lucy asked casually, maybe too casually as Harriet gave her a sharp look.

"They went out for a ride," Charlotte answered first. "I think they wanted time to themselves before all the guests get here."

Planning for the house party diverted Harriet again. She was fretting about the meals and planned activities. Lady Aversley had allowed Harriet to do the bulk of the arrangements for the party, conceding that as the future Lady Aversley, it would soon be her duty and she must learn to act as hostess. But the dowager kept a sharp eye on the preparations and Harriet fretted about her future mother-in-law's oversight.

Lucy slumped as she ate her breakfast. With the house party guests about and Harriet in her bed, there was no way to meet with Aubrey again. Her affair was over before it had barely started. She regretted not taking advantage of her time in London better, but perhaps it was for the best. Her poor heart would not recover quickly from this affair, and she did not have the leisure to collapse into her bed now as she had done the first time.

"Are you done with your breakfast?" Harriet inquired. "I don't mean to hurry you, but the morning will fly by, and people will arrive after lunch." Charlotte rolled her eyes at Lucy behind Harriet's shoulder, but both women arose from the table and followed Harriet down to the sitting room she had made her own for organizing the party.

Every day Harriet was becoming more comfortable with her next position as Baroness of the estate. She was the daughter of an Earl even if her father had been a dissolute roué. He had ignored his daughter as Harriet grew up, leaving her with her governess who ensured that Harriet knew how to run a household and be fit for the role she would one day assume. So even though she had everything planned down to the last detail, Harriet would leave nothing to chance. It was up to Lucy and Charlotte to ensure that all of her wishes were carried out as she had planned.

AUBREY HAD SPENT MOST of his ride with George looking for a folly or gazebo where he could meet with Lucy. George had mentioned that Blakesley was arriving with the other guests today and Aubrey would henceforth share his room with him. This was not unusual at a house party, especially for just a few nights, but Blakesley was a gossip, and they could not trust his discretion if Aubrey were not in his bed at any point during the night. While he did not have to sleep with Lucy, although he was half-aroused at the thought, he needed to spend time with her. Aubrey was not sure when she intended to return to Yorkshire. If he could persuade her to remain in London after the wedding, he would relax more about the next few days. Even better if he could convince her to wed, he would procure a special license at once.

However, if she planned to leave after the wedding, it was critical that he be able to spend more time with her now. Aubrey would follow her to Yorkshire, but he could not depend on being able to see her frequently there unless he made sure of her during the next few days. Aubrey thought he had made good gains last night and his body tensed at the thought of some of those efforts. Making love to Lucy had been all he remembered and more.

They returned to the house, and Aubrey still had not found a place to tryst. Maybe Lucy had an idea if he could even get her alone long enough to ask. The house party and the wedding plans were interfering with his personal plans to seduce Lucy into marriage. George and Aubrey walked into the front hallway where Harriet was directing servants to take luggage away and greeting early guests. The house party would be a small group meant to distract and entertain the bridal couple for the few days before the wedding. The larger group of guests would arrive in two days for the wedding ball, and the wedding ceremony and breakfast the following morning. Many would stay in various inns and estates in the surrounding area. Thornton, for example, would arrive with a party who were staying with him at his nearby house.

George went to his fiancée, and Aubrey walked into the drawing room where he found Lucy and Charlotte sitting at a table with papers spread out in front of them. The women looked up, and Charlotte greeted him amicably. Lucy looked, her brown eyes wide and cheeks pink as she bit her lip. She seemed so unsure of him. Aubrey wished that he could go to her and show her how free from any doubt she should be. Instead, he joined them at the table, pulling his chair just a little closer to Lucy. Under the table, he nudged her leg with his own, and she smiled shyly while he pretended to pay heed to Charlotte explaining about some elaborate entertainment she had planned for the evening.

Lucy slipped her hands into her lap as Charlotte pointed at her papers and made notes. Aubrey discreetly hooked his little finger with hers, and Lucy's smile grew bigger which made him grin.

Charlotte broke off her talking and looked with suspicion at him, so he straightened in his chair and tried to behave.

"Please go on, Lady Charlotte. It sounds fascinating." Aubrey nodded his head, and Lucy suppressed a giggle.

Charlotte narrowed her eyes, not at all reassured. She continued explaining the various games she was planning. Aubrey nodded at appropriate moments but stole glances at Lucy. He frequently caught her looking back, and he felt his heart expand. Aubrey wanted to declare himself right there, go down on one knee and make her his own. Lawd, he sounded like an imbecile, but he had longed for Lucy for so long. He had to wait just a little while longer.

There was a clatter in the hallway, and they all looked towards the doorway. The women both stood and started for the entrance, but Aubrey stayed where he was. Maybe Lucy would return, and he could talk to her with no one else around.

Instead, he heard the rumble of a male voice and Blakesley walked in the door.

"Lady Harriet said you might be in here." As he came closer, he lowered his voice. "Dying of ennui yet?"

"Not at all. The company so far has been amusing and the country tranquil." Aubrey took Blakesley's hand, and they shook. "How are you doing, Harry?"

"Truth to tell I am bored, Lovell. I am ready to retire to my estate just to get away from town for a while. I am glad the season is winding down as I'm tired of avoiding the young ladies and their mothers, tired of the routs and balls. I am even tired of the hells and clubs." Blakesley sat and adjusted the cuffs on his jacket. "I am in a proper snit," he huffed.

One eyebrow went up, but Aubrey didn't respond. Harry Wilton, Lord Blakesley, was a man-about-town, and he doubted that Blakesley would stay in this mood for long. A few days at home with his meddling mother and rambunctious siblings would send him hurrying back to town fast.

Blakesley sat back and studied Aubrey. This was not good. A bored Blakesley caused trouble.

"Got slapped again lately?" he drawled.

"Why no, I have not." Aubrey's eyes flashed a warning which Blakesley ignored.

"I saw the lovely Lady Lucilla fluttering behind Lady Harriet in the hallway. So, you have mended your differences, have you?"

Aubrey snorted; Lucy had never fluttered a day in her life. "We have resolved our differences," was all he would say.

"She is pretty in a rural sort of way, her hair all blowsy like a milkmaid." Blakesley tapped a finger against his lips, waiting for Aubrey to respond. But Aubrey kept his face still, not betraying by a movement that his temper was on the rise. One never wanted to give Blakesley an opening. Yes, he was a friend, but he liked to rattle the cages.

Blakesley nodded. "Well, perhaps I will find amusement here."

Chapter Eighteen

Lucy waited in the drawing room with the rest of the house party for dinner to be announced. Aubrey had entered after her but Lady Charlotte and two other young ladies she did not recognize waylaid him. He had sent her a beseeching look, but he was too much the gentleman to abandon the young ladies. Or at least that was what Lucy hoped.

She had wanted to spend time with him during the day, but there was not a chance to even talk except for brief pleasantries as they passed each other. All the invited guests had arrived, and they had moved Harriet's things into her room. Harriet was all nervous chatter as they prepared for the evening, her maid helping both the women with their hair and dresses.

Harriet was moving around the room, ensuring that her guests had what they needed. She was quite composed, much different from earlier, the perfect hostess and even George's mother looked proud of Harriet's graciousness and tact. She would make George an excellent wife. If he ran for a Parliamentary seat, Harriet would assist him every step of the way.

The butler announced that dinner was ready. Lucy rose but dawdled, hoping that Aubrey would make his way over to where she was standing. If he escorted her into the dining room, then he would sit next to her, and they could converse during dinner. Lucy was famished for his company. There were only a few more days until she left for home and she wanted every minute with him she could get.

Her face fell as she saw one of the young ladies take a firm hold of his arm. He did not even glance at her as he led the young woman into the dining room.

"My lady, may I escort you into dinner?"

Lucy looked up startled. Lord Blakesley stood at her side, his arm out to lead her after the others. Lucy took his arm and walked with him, allowing him to seat her, and she spread her napkin when he sat down next to her. Lady Charlotte was on her other side, and Aubrey sat further down the table on the opposite side, a lovely young lady on either side of him. Lucy looked away as a pang went through her. Apparently, he finished with her and was moving on to greener pastures, perhaps inspecting the field for an eligible wife.

Blakesley gave her a charming smile. Lucy smiled back and looked down, adjusting her napkin. When men attempted to seduce her, they gave her a similar look. But Blakesley was Aubrey's friend, so that seemed unlikely unless Aubrey had agreed to pass her off to his friend. She sneaked another look down at Aubrey, but he was conversing with the woman on his left.

"Are you enjoying yourself, Lady Lucilla?" Blakesley's smooth baritone demanded her attention.

"Of course, my lord. I cannot wait for the wedding day festivities." How true that was, so this could all be over, Lucy thought. "Lady Harriet will be the perfect wife for Baron Aversley, and I believe they will be happy together."

"I suppose. It was fated that old Aversley would be the first of our group to get leg-shackled." Blakesley snorted as if the idea appalled him and Lucy eyed him askance. He unfolded his napkin, making a business of it and looked about the table.

"I suppose that Lovell will be the next to find a wife. Ever since he returned from the Continent, his mother has been busy looking for the next Viscountess."

Lucy tensed but gave a small laugh. "He is also looking judging by the young ladies he escorted into dinner. Do you know who either of them is?"

"The young lady in the pink is Miss Reston. And Lady Ophelia Churchdale has dark hair."

Aubrey had always liked brunette-haired women. Lady Ophelia was the woman he had escorted into the dining room.

"And yes, Lady Ophelia is eligible, niece to the Earl of Shrewsbury." Blakesley seemed to enjoy himself, happy to indulge in gossip. "Miss Reston is not as up to snuff, but her dowry is sizable, trade you know. Lady Lovell would welcome either of the young ladies into her family I am sure if she did not already have someone else picked out."

Lucy still had said nothing, happy to let Blakesley ramble on. She looked up at him, quirked an eyebrow, and waited for him to speak.

"Lady Clarissa, the Duke of Clairmont's daughter, is the chosen one. She will do well enough for Lovell and keep him on the straight and narrow. It will be a bloody dull life for him though." Blakesley seemed to recollect that he was at a dinner party and not his club and he sat up, his cheeks reddening.

"Your pardon, Lady Lucilla. I did not mean to speak so freely." Blakesley looked around, but he had spoken quietly enough that no one else seemed to hear him. Lucy nodded, but it distracted her, thinking about what he said. He turned to talk to the elderly lady on his other side and left Lucy alone for the moment. Her dinner partner still occupied Charlotte, so Lucy pondered his words.

It should not hurt so much, confirmation of the news that Aubrey was seeking a wife., she had expected it. Indeed, she had thought he might have married while he was away. It was a shock he hadn't brought home a wife, a dark-haired Contessa from Italy. And he needed heirs. Her stomach clenched, and she looked at her plate uneasily, not hungry in the least.

Somehow Lucy made it through the meal. Blakesley moved onto other topics, and Charlotte was amusing when she turned to her. Lucy would not look up the table to where Aubrey sat. She pretended that she had no interest in his behavior. Their affair had been regrettably short, but satisfactory as Lucy was returning to Yorkshire soon, anyway. He could marry and for that matter find himself another mistress, one who suited him better than she did.

The ladies rose and retired to the sitting room, leaving the gentlemen to their port. Harriet came over to check on her, but then bustled off to ensure the servants had set up the room correctly. She was planning musical entertainments from the young ladies. Lucy thought of trying to excuse herself from the evening, claiming an upset stomach, but she did not have the heart to leave Harriet, even though she was managing perfectly fine. She took a chair in a corner and watched as the other ladies chatted with each other.

When the gentlemen came in, she watched for Aubrey out of the corner of her eye. He appeared to be looking for someone, but Miss Reston approached him and practically dragged him over to a settee at the front of the room. Lucy gave a sniff. Miss Reston was part of the evening's entertainment and wanted her new beau to have a front-row seat. The only consolation to Lucy was that Lady Ophelia had a sour look on her face, her plans spoiled by the upstart Reston girl who had neatly cut her prey out of the herd and carried him away with her.

"All by yourself, Lady Lucilla. We cannot have that, can we?" Lord Blakesley was back.

"Oh yes we can," thought Lucy, but she put up no demur when he seated himself on a chair next to her as Harriet stood up at the front of the room, her future mother-in-law at her side, to announce the first pianist. They had dragooned Lady Charlotte into displaying her talents. Luckily she played well.

Lucy listened to Charlotte and the young ladies that followed, occasionally nodding her head when Blakesley whispered something to her even though she was not paying him any heed.

When Miss Reston had her turn at the piano, the woman coyly urged Aubrey to assist her by turning the music pages. Lucy was happy to see that Aubrey acted reluctantly and followed the woman to the front of the room because of his good manners. The woman played mechanically with no feeling for the music, and the applause was tepid. Then it was Lucy's turn.

She stepped to the piano where Aubrey waited with a smile on his face.

"Let me assist you with your music, Lady Lucilla."

"No need, thank you." She sat and arranged her skirts while Aubrey bowed and went back to his seat. Then she bent her head over the keys and played. She was playing Beethoven's Piano Sonata No. 8, a piece she loved and knew by heart.

When Lucy played, she only knew the music. Constant practice had enhanced a natural talent for the piano in the last several years. The piano was where her cares fell away, and Lucy played both naturally and beautifully.

When she finished, she placed her hands on her lap and slowly came back to herself. The people in the room stayed quiet and then broke into uproarious applause. Blakesley stood, calling "Bravo" and others took up his cry.

Lucy looked straight at Aubrey. He looked stunned and was clapping languidly as if he could not force his hands to move. She nodded at him and rose, going back to her seat, ignoring the pleas for an encore.

Lady Ophelia then stepped forward, the last to perform.

"Lord Lovell, may I ask for your help with the pages."

Aubrey rose, and Miss Reston sat with her lips pursed, now the unhappy one. Lady Ophelia arranged her music and played, Aubrey leaning over to turn the page. She was a competent musician but after Lucy's performance sounded bland and amateurish. Aubrey's eyes kept wandering toward Lucy, but she did not see him. She focused on the back of the chair in front of her. Blakesley, however, saw where Aubrey's attention was and made a point of dipping his head towards Lucy to murmur in her ear. Aubrey was so incensed with his erstwhile friend he almost missed a page turn, and Lady Ophelia looked up at him reproachfully.

Once Lady Ophelia had taken her bows, Lucy rose and made her way to the door, determined to retire for the night. She moved so quickly that Blakesley did not even realize she was gone until he turned. By then Lucy was walking through the doorway on her way out of the room. He followed and was behind her when she started up the stairs.

"Lady Lucilla, where are you going?"

She stiffened but turned. "Lord Blakesley, I am tired and ready to retire to my room." She turned back to ascend the stairway, but he stepped up and took her arm.

"Please let me escort you, my dear."

"Thank you, but I don't want to take you away from the other guests. I am fine on my own." Lucy pulled her arm away and moved up the staircase.

"I insist." Blakesley was not sure why he was so insistent, but he had had a little too much to drink and determined to follow her.

"The lady does not need your escort."

Blakesley turned to find Aubrey in the middle of the hallway, his face implacable. Lucy never stopped but disappeared at the top of the stairs.

Aubrey watched her then turned back to his friend.

"Why the sudden interest in Lady Lucilla, Blakesley?"

Blakesley blinked and affected surprise. "Why not? The lady is unattached and perhaps willing to indulge in a liaison."

"She most definitely is not either unattached nor did she appear to be willing."

Blakesley narrowed his eyes. "Why should you care? I thought you were wife-hunting."

"I am. Stay away from Lady Lucilla."

Blakesley stepped back down to the hallway, puzzled by his friend's attitude.

"Do you have designs on her?"

Aubrey drew in a deep breath, trying to suppress the urge to use fisticuffs on his old friend. "As you said, I am wife-hunting."

Eyes opened in surprise, Blakesley put his hands up in supplication, recognizing the seriousness of his tone and Aubrey's evident need to pummel him.

"Then excuse me. I did not realize your intent, and I apologize for any offense." He gave a short bow, then strode past Aubrey back into the drawing room.

Aubrey looked up the stairs but knew he had lost any chance of speaking to Lucy that evening. Others would leave to find their bedrooms. He looked back into the drawing room, then went down the hall to the library, hoping to find a book to take back to his room and lull him to sleep. Aubrey feared that he would be up half the night with thoughts of Lucy. He marveled at her competency and artistry at the piano. The Lucy he remembered could play, often with some brilliance, but did not care to practice. She would instead run wild outside in the meadows and woods of her father's estate. But he looked forward to discovering more of the changes that had overtaken the girl he once knew and intended to know well once more.

Chapter Nineteen

Aubrey left the breakfast room just as Miss Reston and Lady Camilla entered. Both young ladies looked disappointed, but they sat down on either side of Blakesley much to his apparent dismay. Lucy had not been at breakfast, and Aubrey determined to find her this morning and spend time talking with her. The days had flown by, and he was out of time. His time with Lucy had proved scant, filled with activities for the guests and errands for George. Aubrey had been unsuccessful in eluding the determined young ladies at the party, and the wedding ball was this evening.

He headed towards the small sitting room that Harriet had been using as her headquarters, but no one was there. Next, he tried the library, but again the room was empty. He wandered towards the front hallway, hoping that someone there might have the information he sought. Harriet was talking to the housekeeper and Aubrey breathed a sigh of relief. Surely where Harriet was today, Lucy would be nearby.

Aubrey waited impatiently for Harriet to finish. She eyed him curiously but continued to converse with Mrs. Johnson, giving final instructions for room preparations. Aubrey mused that Harriet was already making an excellent Baroness although she didn't yet wear the title. It must please the staff that George's mother had ceded her responsibilities, as she was a dragon and Harriet would prove much easier to deal with.

"Good morning Lord Lovell. How may I be of service?"

"Good morrow to you, Lady Harriet. I was looking for Lady Lucilla. I wondered if you had seen her this morning."

Harriet smiled. "She has gone off to the church in the village to supervise the placement of the floral arrangements and ribbons for the wedding morning." Harriet dimpled prettily, thinking about the wedding ceremony that would change her life. "I expect that you might find her there."

Aubrey bowed, then strode off. The walk to the village was only about five minutes and the morning was beautiful. There was a path that was shorter through the woodlands, but he thought Lucy would stay on the main drive and he did not want to bypass her.

The church was not far, on the outskirts of the small village. He walked up to the old wooden doors of the gray stone church and peeked into the dim interior. There were a few women hanging ribbons on the pews, so he stepped inside and looked around, but did not see Lucy anywhere.

"Excuse me, is Lady Lucilla about?"

One woman started and turned to see who was addressing them. She lived in the village, but she recognized the name.

"Lady Lucilla just left a few minutes ago to go back to the big house. We said we would finish up here."

Aubrey thanked them and went back out into the sunshine. He looked up the street but did not see Lucy anywhere. She must have taken the wooded path back to the manor, so he had missed her.

Heaving a sigh, Aubrey retraced his steps back to the manor house. How could it be so hard to track down one woman? Just as he reached the gate, a carriage pulled by a beautiful quartet of matching chestnut horses turned in, raising a small cloud of dust. He cursed to himself and beat at his coat, attempting to remove the grime from his clothing. The coach stopped just a short way up the drive. He looked up to see his mother poke her head out of a window.

"Lovell, why are you walking there?" Her lips were pursed together, denoting her disapproval of his audacity in exercising his limbs on an excellent day.

"Good day to you, mother," he responded dryly. "I did not expect to see you today."

She harrumphed and drew her head inside as he came even with the coach. "Say your how-do's to Lady Clarissa," she grumbled.

Aubrey nodded as his heart sank to his stomach. Why were they there? Well, he knew why his mother was there and why she had brought Lady Clarissa. She intended to force him into marriage. But why did Lady Clarissa put up with her? The daughter of a duke and a diamond of the first water could do better than a mere Viscount. And he was having a hard enough time of it trying to find Lucy without two more obstacles in his way.

Lady Clarissa smiled. "They invited us to dinner before the ball this evening. Since we're staying at my father's estate at Rustling Park nearby, we came over early to help dear Lady Harriet." She blushed enticingly, but Aubrey was in no mood for fatuous young ladies.

"Climb into the carriage, Lovell. Ride with us up to the house as befits your station."

Aubrey looked up the drive hoping to spy Lucy emerging from the woods, but there was no escape there. He opened the coach door and stepped in, seating himself opposite the ladies.

"The Duke will arrive later as he had business to attend to. He will be glad to speak with you this evening." Lady Lovell narrowed her eyes at him. Aubrey thought if she could have got away with kicking him in the shin to make her point, she would have. It was plain what the Duke wanted to speak about, and Aubrey had no intention of obliging him.

"It will be a delight to greet his Grace," he murmured, not committing himself.

The carriage jolted to a halt, and his mother fussed at her skirts, not willing to complain about the Duke's coachman in front of his daughter. Aubrey stepped out and turned to help the ladies step down. Lady Clarissa took his arm with a proprietary air, and he almost jerked it away, but remembered his manners and led her into the house.

Harriet was waiting with her butler and housekeeper and other servants.

"Lady Lovell! Lady Clarissa! I did not expect you this early, but you are most welcome."

His mother swept past him and took Harriet's hands. "Of course, my dear. We came to aid you in this trying time. Your own dear mother was a great friend of mine, and I know that she would want me to do all I can to help you prepare for your wedding ball."

It was all Aubrey could do not to roll his eyes. Harriet's mother had died at her birth, and as far as he knew, his own mother had never exerted herself for Harriet before this moment. But Harriet took it all with aplomb, nodding her head and making arrangements with her housekeeper for the unexpected guests. They would not have to accommodate them for the night, but they would need to find facilities where the two women could rest and use to change for the ball.

Just then Lucy entered the hallway from the sitting room. She stopped short as she saw Lady Lovell, then looked at Aubrey standing behind his mother. He was so glad to see her he forgot Lady Clarissa still hanging on his arm like a limpet until Lucy looked away, her eyes unresponsive.

"Come and sit while I have tea brought to us." Harriet looked at the housekeeper while herding her unexpected guests into the drawing room. She was too polite to shoo them away, but it was clear that she wished them anywhere but here.

Aubrey observed Lucy, ready to bolt after her if she tried to disappear again, but she obediently followed Harriet into the room. So he led Lady Clarissa after them. Once he had her seated, he left her and walked across the room to where Lucy sat in a chair in the corner.

"I am glad to find you," he murmured.

"Lovell, come and entertain us. Lady Clarissa would like to hear more about your time on the Continent." Lady Lovell smiled, but her eyes were hard as she beckoned to him.

Aubrey stood where he was, determined not to leave Lucy to escape him again, but before he could say so, he heard her speak. "Lord Lovell is most entertaining. I'm sure he has many...," she paused, "anecdotes to share with you, especially Lady Clarissa." He choked at the innuendo and gave her a sharp glance while Lucy returned a saucy grin.

"Yes, please do, Lord Lovell. I love to hear your stories." Lady Clarissa was triumphant, and he had no choice, but to sit next to her on the couch while Harriet poured their tea.

Aubrey answered Lady Clarissa's questions and the prompts by his mother, but he never took his eyes from Lucy, who sat in her corner, amused by the attention displayed by the women. Harriet fidgeted, not wanting to offend her guests, but having much to do this day to prepare for the ball. Finally, she interrupted.

"Perhaps you ladies would like to retire to rest and refresh yourselves before dinner and the ball?"

Lady Lovell protested but allowed Harriet to lead them from the room. Lady Clarissa gave Lucy a dark look as she passed her, but changed it to a simpering smile when she looked back at Aubrey, who had declined to escort them. Lucy barely refrained from rolling her eyes and sat silently, waiting to see what Aubrey would do or say.

He cocked an eyebrow and said with a smirk, "Lady Lucilla, you have absented yourself from my presence and I am very displeased with you because of it."

Lucy beamed up at him. "Indeed sir, that was not my intention. But I have been exceedingly busy helping Lady Harriet prepare for the ball. And it would appear that you have found other entertainments to amuse yourself." She folded her hands in her lap, acting demure.

"A gentleman may not and cannot respond to that remark." He held out a hand. "Would you walk with me, Lucy?"

She rose and took his arm, happy to have his heat and masculine scent at her side.

"Not that way," he demurred, showing the hallway where obstructions might still lurk. "Let us try the side door." He led her to the attached conservatory where they passed outside onto the wide lawn and gardens. Aubrey picked up his pace when he saw the wide windows of the small ballroom that George's mother had built onto the main house, hoping to avoid the hordes of servants working in the room, readying it for the night's festivities. He led Lucy towards a small copse of wood at the far side of the gardens. When they had gone a few feet into the woods, far enough he could no longer see the house, Aubrey stopped and turned to Lucy.

"At last! I have been desperate to see you, be with you," Aubrey murmured as he backed Lucy against a broad old oak. He set her against the bark with his hands on her shoulders.

She looked away nervously. "I did not even bring my hat."

He barked out a sharp laugh and let the back of one hand caress her cheek. "Oh Lucy, I have missed you. I cannot wait until this damned wedding is over and done with so I can have you for myself."

"What do you mean? I must go home next week as I have responsibilities, people who depend on me." Lucy pushed against his chest, but Aubrey did not move. "I told you that this, whatever we're doing, would only last until the wedding is over. Then I must go home."

"I never agreed to that."

Lucy stopped pushing and looked up in surprise. "Whatever do you mean?"

"I have plans for us, and nothing you say or do will change that."

"Aubrey, you abandoned me five years ago, but my life did not stop. I have changed, and you have changed." Her pulse was fluttering in panic and excitement.

"But I still love you, and you still love me, that has not changed. We can manage the rest." Aubrey heaved a deep breath. "Be with me always, Lucy. I love you."

Lucy felt her distress fly away, drifting over the trees. He was right, they would work it out after they married. But...

"Yes, then, yes. But Aubrey, there is something I must tell you that can't wait..."

His mouth interrupted her, and her lips opened as his tongue plundered her depths. He held her face, careful not to push her too hard against the tree, but not willing to release her. Lucy's arms slid up around his neck and pulled him closer. He broke away from her mouth and kissed his way down the side of her neck.

"What... oh," Lucy gasped.

Lucy did not care whether the bark scratched against her back or if someone heard them from the house. She wanted Aubrey to make love to her. The fire had blazed so fast between them. She closed her eyes as he took her over the edge and then followed her there. Aubrey balanced one hand against the tree and held onto Lucy with the other, somehow keeping them both standing.

Lucy caught her breath and shakily adjusted her clothes, brushing pieces of bark away from her dress.

"Did I hurt you? I lost control of myself." Aubrey grimaced.

"No, I am fine, but I need to get back to the house. Harriet will wonder where I am."

"Go. I will wait a moment, then follow you." She gave him a quick smile and a kiss and then walked swiftly away. Aubrey grinned as he waited. Lucy had agreed, she was to be his.

Chapter Twenty

Lucy watched as George led Harriet out for the first dance of the wedding eve ball. Harriet was radiant in a lovely pink dress that matched the blush on her cheeks. George was beaming at his bride-to-be in a manner that left no doubt of his feelings for her.

Aubrey was across the room, standing with his friend Blakesley. He looked very handsome in his formal clothes.

She nervously smoothed the silk of her skirt. Harriet had insisted that she buy a new dress for the ball and she had a dressmaker make it up when she was in London. The blue was so light it appeared an iridescent-tinted white. She wore the pearl eardrops that Lady Wakefield had given her for her come out. Harriet had said she looked like an ice queen, but Lucy liked the effect against the richness of her dark hair. She hoped Aubrey admired the dress.

Thinking back to the afternoon, Lucy blushed. What had she been thinking to make love with him outside like that? Anyone could have come upon them. True, they were planning to marry, but she did not want more scandal.

Others had joined Harriet and George on the dance floor now. Lucy moved to a corner where she could sit in peace. Aubrey had spoken for two dances later in the evening, but she expected no one else to ask her to dance except for perhaps George. Lucy settled in to watch, trying to keep an eye on any possible mishaps before Harriet could see and panic. But George's staff was excellent, and there was nothing for her to do at this point.

Therefore, Blakesley startled Lucy when he appeared and asked her to dance. She rose and put her hand in his, and he led her to the floor. Aubrey was in the set dancing with Lady Charlotte. He gave her a warm smile but narrowed his eyes at Blakesley, who ignored him.

"It seems a pity that your swain has not asked for your hand in a dance, my lady," Blakesley said.

"My swain?"

"Lovell, of course."

"Lord Lovell is not my swain, although he *has* put his name on my card for two dances this evening." Lucy twirled around Blakesley, and he turned to face her once again and raised her hand to promenade down the set. When they reached the end of the row, they waited for the next couple.

"I stand corrected then." When Lucy lifted an eyebrow in question to his statement, he continued. "Lovell has shown his evenhandedness by asking you for two dances. He shares his favors impartially."

"I know not your meaning, my lord."

"No matter. I'm sure he will make it clear soon enough." Blakesley stepped forward to turn her, but Lucy was still pondering his words. There was a ripping sound as he stepped on her dress before she could move away. She looked down in dismay.

"I apologize, Lady Lucilla. It is entirely my fault." Blakesley's face was red as he surveyed the damage done to her dress.

"It's not too bad. I will go to the retiring room and have it mended. It was not your fault," Lucy murmured although she was distressed by the small rip in her beautiful dress. Blakesley escorted her to the hallway where she left him to enter the morning room was in use as a retiring room for the evening. Maids were waiting to assist the ladies and Lucy went over behind a screen to undress so that a maid could mend the rip in her hem. Other ladies were using the mirrors or going behind the screens to find a chamber pot. Lucy handed out her dress to a clucking servant girl and settled down to wait until her gown was ready.

Most of the noise in the room subsided as women left to return to the ballroom.

"We will announce the marriage as soon as they complete the settlements and they are signed," a woman's voice near to her said. Lucy did not mean to, but waiting bored her, so she peeked to see through the gap in the screen where it folded. It was Lady Lovell, Aubrey's mother. Had Aubrey spoken to her about their marriage already? It seemed unlikely, but she did not sound displeased. Lucy expected her son's choice of a wife to upset her future mother-in-law. And who was she speaking to?

"I wish he would show a little more enthusiasm. I realize that this is a business arrangement, but he seems oblivious. We have to make a good show of it."

Lucy leaned a little further to see that the other speaker was Lady Clarissa, sitting in front of a mirror while Lady Lovell hovered behind her.

The maid came behind the screen with her dress, and there Lucy stood with her mind in a whirl. She could not think what the two women were speaking of. The maid arranged the gown around her and stepped back.

"It looks fine even if I say so myself, my lady. You can't even see the tear."

"Yes, thank you so much." Lucy did not even look down at the mended hem but walked around the screen. Lady Lovell looked and at once turned away, giving her the cut direct. Lady Clarissa, however, studied Lucy's reflection in her mirror.

"I suppose you heard us talking." She turned to face Lucy, looking her up and down. "It does not matter you know. Lovell may have you as his mistress, but I will be his wife and bear his children, his legitimate children anyway." Lady Clarissa turned back to her mirror dismissing

Lucy. Lady Lovell's shoulders were shaking, and her back was rigid. Lucy straightened her own spine and swept by the two women without ever saying a word.

Once in the corridor, she turned away from the ballroom intent on finding refuge. She needed to clear her mind and understand what had just happened. The library was empty, so she closed the door behind her and sat in the chair behind the desk that George used for his estate work.

Lucy placed both palms flat on the desk in front of her and took a deep breath. What did Lady Clarissa mean? It sounded as if she was marrying Aubrey, but he was marrying Lucy! Or was he? She sat back, thinking over what they had said to each other that afternoon.

He had just mentioned being together forever, but he had never actually asked her to marry. She had just assumed that was what he meant. Was Lady Clarissa correct? Was he going to marry the suitable choice and keep Lucy as his mistress?

Her heart hurt, and she put both hands over her chest and rubbed, trying to erase the pain. Lucy blinked back tears. This was worse than before when he had abandoned her and gone to Italy. By not choosing her as his wife he was leaving her all over again. She clenched her fists and sank her chin upon them to think.

After a long while, Lucy straightened and let out a sigh. She had made her plans. Harriet would aid her, and she would understand what Lucy had to do, once she explained to her. She nodded to herself and rose, head held high. She would not break down now; that could come later.

Lucy swept into the ballroom, a small smile pasted onto her face. She made her way over to the refreshment table, nodding at people as she passed them even when she did not know who they were. She accepted a glass of punch from the footman stationed at the punch bowl and turned to survey the room. Her heart was pounding, but she did not think anyone would notice her anxiety. In her pale blue dress and with her white skin, she was the epitome of an ice queen.

She spotted Aubrey as he made his way around the edge of the room coming towards her. It was near time for their first dance. She steeled herself and lifted her chin in greeting.

"Lady Lucilla, I have been looking for you. I believe this is our dance, is it not?"

His golden eyes were warm, but Lucy reminded herself it was merely lust she detected.

"Of course, my lord. Will you lead me out?"

She offered her hand, and he swept her onto the floor in a waltz. Aubrey pulled her closer, and she tried not to react.

"My lady, have I told you how beautiful you look tonight?"

"Thank you, my lord. And you are quite dashing tonight."

"Just tonight?" Aubrey was in a teasing mood.

"Well, aren't we full of ourselves?" Lucy's tone was a little sharper than she wished and Aubrey shot her a confused glance.

"Are you enjoying yourself, Lucy? I thought to see you dancing more."

"I almost never dance at balls." She did not bother to explain that only rakes or her brother's friends ever asked her to dance and there were neither here tonight. Aubrey expertly twirled her, moving around another couple.

"You should dance through life, Lucy. Your path should be a map of stars and light to lead you to every happiness."

She laughed. "You are poetic, my lord. But I am content with my life as it is." That was the only warning he would receive from her, subtle but mayhap he would remember it later.

"Oh no, Lucy. Life will be so much better for both of us. Finally! I cannot wait."

She inclined her head and curtsied as the dance ended.

"Would you like refreshments, my lady?"

"No, thank you, I had a glass of punch before you presented yourself. I am content to sit now."

"Sit, Lucy? No, I must find you a partner. I wish there were not this stupid convention or I would dance with you every dance." Aubrey was looking around the room seeking Blakesley or another acquaintance to squire her. "Perhaps I should dance with you again, anyway."

"No Aubrey, that is unnecessary. I don't want to make a scene."

Lady Lovell swept up to her son and took his arm. "Lovell, please come with me. Lady Clarissa is without a partner for this dance."

Aubrey stood his ground not bothering to hide his exasperation. "And why is that my problem, mother?"

Lady Lovell shot a glance at Lucy and said smoothly, "Her father, the Duke, is detained and I promised him she would be properly attended on tonight. It would not do for her to have to dance with one of the local men. The daughter of a Duke should be treated according to her station."

Aubrey rolled his eyes and turned to Lucy. "You will be all right here?"

Lucy looked past him to Lady Lovell. "Of course, I will." The woman had the grace to redden but said not a word as she tugged her son away.

Lucy watched as Aubrey bowed to Lady Clarissa and led her out in a country dance. She was beautiful, her dress ivory and with sapphires at her neck and ears. Her blonde hair was piled up in curls with sapphire pins peeking out. They made a distinguished couple, Aubrey with his darker locks while she was so fair. Lucy watched for a long moment and then turned to find Harriet.

Chapter Twenty-One

The wedding had gone off without a hitch. Harriet was now Lady Aversley, smiling shyly at one and all while George beamed beside her. Aubrey had done his duty by standing up with George, all the while wishing it were he and Lucy standing before the pastor. It would not be long before that scenario played out if he had his way. Lucy had looked beautiful standing near the bride to bear witness to the union.

He moved out into the sunshine with Lucy on his arm. A faint whiff of vanilla teased his senses, and he glanced at her, but she was concentrating on Harriet and George.

"They look so happy," she said somewhat wistfully.

"They are. Are you jealous? Don't be, it won't be long before we are together."

Lucy looked up at him, her eyes solemn under the brim of her bonnet. "Do you really think we could be that happy?"

Aubrey walked her to a corner of the churchyard that was relatively private.

"Lucy, are you unhappy? We are together, and we will continue so no matter what might ensue. I promise you."

"Of course." She blinked and looked away. "I am just a little tired. The last fortnight has been so busy, and Harriet was nervous last night, so I stayed up to talk to her and soothe her."

He gave her a doubtful look, but accepted her words and led her to the carriage waiting for them. They would return to the estate for the wedding breakfast. Most of the guests would depart after that, but he and Lucy were staying for one more night before returning to London.

George and Harriet would have their privacy, and with some luck, he and Lucy could find their own seclusion tonight as well.

Lucy slid across the seat away from him when he followed her into the carriage opposite Harriet and George. He frowned and moved a little closer to her. She wasn't skittish because of George and Harriet. They scarcely noticed anything wrapped up in their own happiness as they were.

Lucy settled her skirts but did not look up at him. Her behavior made Aubrey unsettled. What was the matter? She had been quiet last night and today, even accounting for her participation in the wedding activities. He frowned. Once he got her alone, he would find out what was bothering her.

They waited as George helped Harriet out of the carriage and a great cheer went up from the waiting servants. Then Aubrey assisted Lucy, giving her arm a squeeze as she stepped down on the gravel. She nodded and faced the doorway, keeping an eye on Harriet and George as they passed into the house.

The distance in her manners puzzled Aubrey. It was as if yesterday afternoon had never happened and they were back to when they first met again in London a few weeks ago.

Once they were inside, she stepped to the side to allow other guests to enter the hallway.

"Please excuse me, my lord. I need a short time in private." Lucy blushed, signaling her need for a chamber pot.

"Of course." He watched as she hurried up the stairs. She turned part way up to see him looking after her, and she gave a small wave, then turned and stepped up the rest of the stairway.

Aubrey smiled, reassured by that wave. Lucy would not have made the gesture in public if she had any doubts. She was just exhausted after she had worked so hard to make everything perfect for Harriet.

Satisfied, he strode through the house to the ballroom where tables had been set up for the wedding breakfast. George and Harriet were just taking their seats when he found his place next to George.

"Where is Lucy?" George asked.

"She will be here soon, I am sure," Harriet answered before he could.

"Yes, she had a matter to attend to," he said perplexed, wondering at Harriet's answer. Had she seen Lucy ascend the stairs and come to her own conclusions? He shrugged, hungry and ready for a hearty meal. Assuaging George's nerves this morning had not left time for breakfast, and he was starving.

People were coming and going, some to sit and eat, some to talk to George and Harriet. Time was passing, and Lucy had still not appeared. Some people were already departing the festivities, although he noticed that his mother and her acolyte, Lady Clarissa, were still in attendance. But Lucy had not returned, and Aubrey felt his nerves speed up.

He found his chance and asked Harriet, "Lady Lucilla has not returned. Perhaps I should check on her."

"I am sure she is just fine," Harriet said, lifting a fork full of kippers to her mouth. "You needn't leave your meal. I will have a maid go upstairs and find her."

Aubrey sat back, then glanced at George, who shrugged his shoulders and applied himself to his own meal. Now that the wedding was over he was hungry also, and he had not as much opportunity to eat with the guests addressing him and Harriet. Another neighbor came up to the table and disturbed Harriet once more. She smiled politely and put her fork down, poking George to gain his attention.

Aubrey waited, but he did not see Harriet signal for a maid. He rose once more when Harriet caught him from the corner of her eye. She broke off her conversation and called, "Mary. Can you please come here?"

A maid hurried over, and Harriet whispered into her ear. Once she had sent the maid off, she gave Aubrey a stern look. "Lucy is fine. Mary will find her so stay in your seat please."

Aubrey could not dispute her command as she was the bride, and this was her wedding breakfast, but he was becoming more and more uneasy. Lucy had been gone for quite some time. He thought back to that small wave she had given him on the stairway and his breakfast settled into a cold lump in his stomach. He waited impatiently for Mary to return with Lucy, but when she appeared, she was alone. She hurried over to Harriet and whispered once more.

"Where is she?" Aubrey was trying to speak quietly but his tone was louder than he meant to be and a few people nearby looked up.

"Lady Lucilla will be here soon. There has been a delay."

George sat back, sated from his meal and looked between his new wife and best friend. Something was going on, and he did not like it — especially if it upset Harriet.

"Be at ease, Lovell! Lucy would not miss the entire breakfast."

Aubrey muttered, "She nearly has already." But he subsided back into his chair once more and pushed a piece of bread around his plate as he minded the doorway.

His mother and Lady Clarissa had their heads together. He did not like that either. There was trouble brewing in that corner. He watched warily as his mother rose and approached him.

"Lovell, it is important that I speak to you."

"All right, mother. What is the matter?" Aubrey was tiring of her importunities. He had asked her to go to her sister's home and did not expect nor want to have her dogging his footsteps. He was not angry at her any longer, but he was wary of her machinations.

"In private please." She turned, expecting him to follow, and he sighed but pushed away from the table.

She led him into George's library, a small room with several bookcases and a huge desk that George used for conducting his estate business. There was a chair in front of the desk, but Lady Lovell remained standing, tapping one finger on the polished wood.

"When you return to London tomorrow, you will meet with the Duke of Clairmont to discuss your marriage settlements."

Aubrey blinked but did not betray his surprise in any other way. He was long used to his mother's manipulations, but he was no longer a raw boy who had to concede to her dictates. He was a man who had been on his own for over five years and would make his own decisions.

"Lady Clarissa can do better than a mere Viscount. Even if she is a younger daughter, she is still the daughter of a Duke," he drawled.

"Of course, but Clairmont has the influence to make you an Earl. He will do that for his beloved youngest daughter."

Aubrey remained calm, but he seethed inside. "And Lady Clarissa? What does she get out of this?"

For the first time, his mother looked irritated. "Surely you know it is a brilliant match for her. Lady Clarissa is thrilled by your suit."

"Lady Clarissa does not even know me. And there has been no suit I know of," he responded dryly.

His mother moved around the desk and sat in George's chair. "That is not important. Many marriages start off this way in the Ton. Your father and I were in an arranged marriage, for example."

"And look how well that turned out."

"Do not be snide. This is a great opportunity for both you and the title."

"Mother, I am not marrying Lady Clarissa." Aubrey leaned over the desk, and his mother pushed backward into her chair.

"But we have made the arrangements. You need to look the papers over and sign your name to them."

"The last I knew I was in my majority and have been for some time. You cannot make those decisions or any type of decision for me. I repeat, I am not marrying Lady Clarissa."

His mother sniffed. "I suppose you think to marry that Blount girl. She is a scandal and will heap ruin on your head."

"Lady Lucilla is an honorable and kind lady whom I have loved since my boyhood."

"Then have her for your mistress. That's what your father would have done."

"I am not my father." Aubrey pounded a fist on the desk, and his mother shrank back. He inhaled a breath and calmed himself.

"I am marrying Lady Lucilla Blount, and there is nothing you can do about it." He turned on his heel and started for the door when his mother spoke again.

"And the lady knows of your intentions?"

"Of course."

"Well then, we will see."

Aubrey stopped and turned to stare at her. "What do you mean?"

She rose from the chair. "Nothing, darling. Never mind, I can put the Duke off for a few weeks until you come to your senses."

She walked past him and out the door and Aubrey followed until he reached the ballroom. Lucy was still not in her seat, so he hesitated but a moment and then strode back down the hallway to the main staircase. He took the stairs two at a time past an astonished footman and headed for the corridor where Lucy's bedroom was located. The door was ajar, so Aubrey walked in to find a maid tidying the room.

"Where is Lady Lucilla?" he barked as the poor woman stopped making up the bed, her eyes wide.

"She's gone," the maid quavered.

"Gone where? Did she move to another room?"

"No, my lord, I believe she left the estate directly after the wedding. I packed her bags up last evening."

Aubrey closed his eyes trying to understand what the woman was saying. Had Lucy left for London already? Why had she not spoken to him?

"Did she leave a message?" he asked the poor maid.

"Not with me, my lord. You could check with Lady Harriet, I suppose."

Aubrey nodded and left, determined to find Harriet and understand the matter. He located her in the downstairs hallway with George, saying goodbye to the last of their wedding guests.

He waited impatiently while their conversation dragged on. Aubrey knew Harriet had seen him. She turned pale and edged around, so he was out of her vision. She seemed to clutch George's sleeve rather tightly. The cold feeling in the pit of Aubrey's stomach grew more prominent and settled in under his heart.

Finally, the older couple said their goodbyes and walked out the door. Harriet moved as if to follow them, but George held her in place and laughed.

"You have done your duty, wife. Let them go now. It's time for you to attend to your new husband."

Harriet blushed as she turned back.

"Aubrey! I did not see you standing there," she lied prettily.

"I am sure," he replied with a searching look.

George was in a jovial mood. The wedding had passed, and he had his wife all to himself — mostly. It was plain he was ready for Aubrey to find something else to do for the rest of the day.

"So, it was a beautiful wedding, and all, was it not? But you will have to pardon us as I would like to speak to my new wife." George raised an eyebrow and looked up the stairs, failing in his attempt at discretion.

"Just a minute, George. I am still looking for Lucy. Harriet, do you know where she is?"

"I suppose that she is about here somewhere." Harriet bit her lip.

George looked thoughtful. "I have not seen Lucy since the ride from the ceremony itself. She should have been at breakfast."

"Perhaps she is lying down. She worked hard to help bring this all about." Harriet was tugging at George's sleeve, impatient to be gone.

Aubrey narrowed his eyes. "I was just in her room. A maid is cleaning it up and says she has left the estate. I saw none of her things about."

"Harriet, what do you know? Where is Lucy?" George was acting as the lord of the manor, frowning at his new wife.

Harriet sighed. "She has gone. She needed to leave right after the ceremony."

"Without saying farewell to any of us? That does not sound like Lucy." George was puzzled.

"Where did she go? Is she headed back to London?"

Harriet pouted. "I suppose so. You might find her at the townhouse. She did not really say."

"Or you did not ask so as not to have to lie to us when asked?"

George turned in astonishment at Aubrey's tone, ready to defend his new wife, but Aubrey paid no mind.

Harriet shrugged her shoulders and fiddled with the lace at the front of her dress. A sudden thought struck Aubrey.

"Which coach did she use when she left? She arrived here in yours."

Harriet bit her lip again, and George crossed his arms across his chest, encouraging her to confess.

"Her brother had sent a carriage for her use in her return. She could stay in London for a few days, or she might return north. I do not know."

George put his arm around his new wife and looked at Aubrey. "You are going after her?"

Aubrey nodded, already headed for the stairs to get the essentials packed. "Send whatever I might leave onto my townhouse if you would. I'm leaving for London within the hour."

Chapter Twenty-Two

Aubrey had been riding in the rain for most of the day, and he was soaked to his skin by the time he rode through the gates of Lovell Abbey. It had been a rough several days, and he was weary to the bone. Part of him wanted to ride over to Wakefield Park immediately and beard his elusive quarry in her lair, but he was too tired and wet to go just yet. First, he wanted something hot to eat and a strong brandy to go with it.

He had sent a message from London to let the staff know he would arrive, but he was happy when a stable boy ran out to take his horse.

"Rub him down good and give him a warm mash. He's had a hard few days."

The front door opened as he arrived, Jemison, his butler, taking his coat and hat with a broad smile.

"Welcome home, Master St. Clare, or should I say, Lord Lovell. It is good to see you, sir. It has been far too long since you have been home."

"Thank you, Jemison. I am glad to be home. Everything seems in good order."

"Indeed, sir. Jones, your estate manager, ensures that all runs well on the estate." Jemison handed the wet gear off to a footman. "Your dinner is ready in the dining room when you say the word, my lord."

Aubrey nodded and walked to the dining room without bothering to get further cleaned up. The staff had laid out a meal for him to eat in solitary splendor. There had been few occasions for him to use this room in the past. Before he had left, his parents had considered him too young, and then he had been away at school. On the occasions he was at home, his parents were often away, and so he took his meals in the smaller breakfast room, preferring the atmosphere there.

The room was quiet, the only noise the scrape of a fork on china or the rustle of cloth as a footman poured more wine in his goblet. Aubrey tried to picture Lucy sitting across from him down the long table. His parents had often sat thus, communicating only occasionally. He and Lucy would never be like that. He intended they have a very different type of marriage, one based on love and mutual respect. Of course, that would be only if he could find her and wed her.

He had been delayed in London, hoping to find her there. But the Wakefield townhouse was empty, except for the housekeeper and her husband, once he finally gained admittance on Sunday afternoon. Still, the time spent had been worthwhile, thinking of the special license he had procured. And he would find Lucy tomorrow at her brother's estate. She had nowhere to run from there.

THE DOOR TO WAKEFIELD Hall swung open without a sound. Williams, a tiny Welshman, who had been the butler here as long as Aubrey could remember stood there. Williams recognized him, or perhaps he was expecting Aubrey to turn up if Lucy had alerted him.

He bowed. "Welcome, my lord. How may I serve you?"

Aubrey handed him his hat. "Hello, Williams. It has been a long time. Is your mistress at home?"

"I will have to check to see if the Countess is receiving visitors." He turned away but stopped when Aubrey spoke again.

"Excuse me, I am here to see Lady Lucilla."

Williams turned back to him with a frown but then wiped the expression off his face.

"Just so, sir," With that enigmatic statement, he walked off leaving Aubrey to cool his heels in the hallway.

In just a few minutes Williams was back. "Follow me please."

He led Aubrey into a parlor where Lady Anne was sitting on a settee, her needlework set to her side. She was an attractive blonde and far gone with child.

"Forgive me for not greeting you, my lord. I am limited in my movements at this point."

Aubrey seated himself as a tall, slender man with dark-blonde hair came through the door. He rose to greet the Richard Blount, Earl of Wakefield, Lucy's brother, or rather, half-brother.

"Lovell, welcome home. It has been years since you were in these parts." The Earl was polite, but only had eyes for his Countess, who was smiling at her husband reassuringly.

"Thank you. I am glad to be home again."

"Have you met my Countess? My dear, this is our neighbor, Viscount Lovell, who has just returned from a sojourn in Europe, Italy I believe. Lord Lovell, my wife, Lady Anne."

"I am pleased to meet you, Lady Anne. You have my belated good wishes on your wedding." Aubrey did not mention the expected child, feeling that was too personal. Lady Anne was not so shy.

She smiled and inclined her head. "Would you like refreshments, my lord? I find that I must eat every few hours at this point. It is a wonder I can move from place to place."

"Thank you, my lady. I appreciate your kindness."

The Earl stepped into the hallway and murmured to a footman, then returned and sat by his wife. She patted his hand in thanks, her display of affection noted by Aubrey. Earl Richard and his wife were not afraid to show small exhibitions of tenderness in public.

"How do you find matters over at Lovell Abbey? Your steward seems a good man."

"The estate is in fine shape from what I could see. I only arrived last evening and will meet with him later today."

"You arrived last evening and are paying neighbor visits already? I am honored." The Earl was plainly surprised but too polite to voice it overtly.

"Yes, I had met Lady Lucilla in London, and I was hoping to speak to her this morning if she is available."

The Earl exchanged looks with his wife. "Lady Lucilla is not here. I believe she went to visit friends north of here directly on her return from London."

Aubrey was flabbergasted. At the last posting inn, the hostler had told him that Lucy's coach was headed to Wakefield Park. There had not been enough time for her to change plans or leave again. Lady Anne had her head down, not meeting his eyes, but her husband appeared unconcerned.

Aubrey tried again. "She did not stop at Wakefield Park? Forgive me, but I was sure she would want to rest at home for a few days after her journey and reassure herself as to the health of Lady Anne."

Lady Anne's head sunk even further and she started nervously to rub at her belly.

"No, we received a note she was going further north." The Earl did not appear to wish to discuss his sister's movements any further, but Aubrey persisted.

"Would you know where her friends are staying? She did not indicate that she was undertaking another journey when I last saw her at Lord Aversley's wedding."

Lord Richard's tone was distinctly cool when he answered. "Lady Lucilla is a grown woman and able to guard her own movements. I suppose that if she wanted you to know where she was, she would have told you." Lady Anne winced and reached for his arm, but Aubrey knew when to hold his fire.

"Of course, my lord. I just wanted to ensure that she had concluded her journey safely. I would have traveled with her if she had apprised me of her plans earlier."

The Earl nodded but said nothing further as Williams brought the tea cart into the room. Lady Anne fussed with serving, and the conversation became a general discussion about families in the neighborhood and conditions at the estate farms. Aubrey was thwarted in any further talk about Lucy, and he rose to leave, convinced that the Earl was not telling him everything. His Countess was not in agreement with him, but she would not dispute her husband's word. Aubrey did not think the Earl was lying, but he was concealing something.

Aubrey had been sure that Lucy would be at Wakefield Park and he had not an idea where else she might be hiding. He was not aware of any other friends or relatives who might shelter her, especially further north.

As he rode home, he reflected that Lucy was not far away. If he was any judge, Lady Anne was near her time. Lucy would want to be near so she could be at the Park when the baby arrived. He would have to keep a lookout and contain his impatience. The special license burned a hole in his coat pocket, but it would keep.

The bigger question was why Lucy had fled to begin with? She would not play games with him, he thought, not about this. Had someone, his mother perhaps, said something to make her leave so precipitously? He would get to the bottom of the matter, but meanwhile, he needed to meet with his factor.

Chapter Twenty-Three

Aubrey had been home nearly a week before he received word that Lady Anne was giving birth. He had found a groom in his stable walking out with a maid at Wakefield Park. With persuasion and some coin, he had convinced young Jack to keep him apprised of the goings-on at the Park.

It was late evening when Jack had come to the house to notify Aubrey of the events taking place nearby. Aubrey had ordered his horse at once. Surely Wakefield would summon Lucy for the birth of her nephew or niece.

Aubrey rode straight to Wakefield Park. It was only when he was near that he realized that Aubrey had no idea of what he would do when he arrived. He had no relationship with the Earl or his family that would allow him entrance at such a delicate time. Aubrey could not demand to enter and ask to see Lucy at such a time. The Earl would have him tossed out on his ear.

He headed for the stable still not sure how he should proceed. It was late in the day for a social call even if he tried to pretend that he did not know a birth was in progress. A groom ran out to take his horse, and he swung down.

"Here, my lord, I can take him."

"That's all right. Do you know if the family is at home? I realized that it is rather late in the day for a call."

The groom was young, and his excitement caused him to confide more than a good servant should. "They have called The doctor, and we are waiting for news. A new heir for Wakefield is our hope though we will be happy with a healthy baby."

The boy amused Aubrey. He acted as if he was the proud papa, but the Earl was a good master, and his people were loyal to the family.

"And Lady Lucilla? Has she arrived yet?"

"Oh yes, my lord. She rode in an hour ago. The Earl sent Thomas off to get her. I have got her mare settled down for the night as I expect she will be here for a while."

Aubrey made a quick decision. "Perhaps I should not disturb the family. I'll return in the morning, and hopefully, there will be news then." He swung back up on his horse and leaned down to pass the groom a coin. "No need to bother the family I was here."

The groom tipped his hat while Aubrey rode home. He would deal with Lucy in the morning.

LUCY SAT WITH CARE on the edge of the bed watching her sister-in-law with her new son. Richard stood next to them, his face filled with wonder as he held his son's tiny fingers in his own large hand.

"I think Ned suits him," Anne said, her eyes tired, but a tender smile on her face.

"Edward George Blount is a lovely name." Lucy felt her eyes tearing up at the tableau in front of her. "He is a beautiful baby. I think he will keep his blonde hair and blue eyes, like both his parents."

Anne laughed. "There is not much hair on his head yet."

There was a knock on the door, and Richard moved to answer it. Lucy heard him murmuring to Williams. "I'll speak to her. Meanwhile, keep him downstairs in the small drawing room."

A quiver ran through Lucy. It was very early in the morning, much too soon for callers. She knew from Richard's face that Aubrey had arrived downstairs.

"Lovell is here. He knows you are here and wants to speak to you."

Anne struggled to sit up without disturbing the baby. Richard picked the child up from her as if he had been carrying babies his entire life. Anne leaned forward and took Lucy's hand.

"What will you do? How could he know you were here?"

Lucy grimaced. "I imagine he heard about the baby somehow and knew I would come. But I do not want to see him. He will importune me to return to London, and I do not wish that."

Richard laid the baby in his crib. "I can send him off so he will not bother you again."

"He has been very persistent," Anne said doubtfully. "I'm not sure he will leave until he speaks to Lucy."

"He will leave if I bring several footmen along to greet him." The long night had tired Richard, and he was in no mood to be trifled with.

Lucy huffed out a breath. "I did not mean to bring this trouble to you on this happiest of days. I do not want some sort of fracas to occur."

"Perhaps you should speak to him, Lucy. If you are firm with him, he will leave you alone." Anne picked at her coverlet. "Besides, are you so certain of what he wants? Maybe he desires something else entirely."

"What is it he wants, anyway?" Richard demanded. "I can think of only one reason a man would accost a young lady in her home, and that is marriage. If that is so, why not speak to him?"

Lucy exchanged glances with Anne and sighed. She had not shared everything with her brother. If she told him that Aubrey only wanted her as a mistress, Richard would explode. Although he had a good point. Why would Aubrey expect that he could ask that of her in her family home?

"Lucy? What would you have me do?" Richard distracted her from her thoughts.

Lucy squared her shoulders. "Distract him, please. I will escape out the side and make my way to the stable. If you can give me a quarter hour, I will be away. He only keeps coming here because he does not know where I bide and he cannot be sure that I am here now."

Richard frowned. "I can send him away, Lucilla." He was using his big brother voice, trying to be assertive. Lucy put her hand on his arm.

"He would wait and follow me if you do that. I think it would be better for me to slip away." Lucy kissed Richard on his cheek and then embraced Anne. She walked over to the crib to look at her nephew. "Goodbye, Ned. I will be back soon."

"Very well, let me send Williams up with your cloak and have a footman ensure your mare is ready. I will take Lovell into the breakfast room so you should be able to reach the stables unseen." He shook his head. "But I dislike this, Lucy."

Richard walked away, but stopped and looked back. "You will be careful please, Lucilla."

She nodded her head, unable to speak. He looked past her to his wife. "Rest, love. I will be back as soon as I am able." He left the room.

"He will do anything for you, you know." Anne smiled and put out her hand to draw Lucy to her side. "As will I."

"I know," Lucy whispered.

"But I think you are making a mistake. You should speak to Lovell." Anne paused and then went on. "You love him, and I think he loves you as well. I watched him when he was here looking for you. He is miserable without you."

"That's not the issue. I cannot be his mistress, and he must marry someone whose reputation is not as besmirched as mine."

"That is not true. I think Richard is correct, Lovell would not show himself here if he did not have honorable intentions towards you."

"Then it is even worse." Lucy closed her eyes in pain. "I have not told him yet, Anne. And it will break him when he finds out what I have kept from him. He cannot marry me."

"I think you are wrong in this, Lucy. You should give him a chance."

"I can't. What if he abandons me again? And this time, he could take more than my heart with him."

Anne sighed. "But what if he stays? You could be as happy as Richard and me."

"I cannot chance it." Lucy gave Anne a kiss on the cheek. "I will be back as soon as I can. Meanwhile, please rest and enjoy your motherhood. My new nephew is a sweetheart."

"You will be back for the christening? My son must have his godmother in attendance."

"Of course, I will. I promise."

Lucy slipped through the door and met Williams with her cloak. Within minutes, she had collected her horse from the stables and was off.

Chapter Twenty-Four

Aubrey walked down to the stables highly frustrated. Wakefield had taken him into his breakfast room, all good bonhomie after his long night awaiting the birth of his heir. He insisted on describing the baby in excruciating detail while Aubrey pushed a piece of toast around his plate.

Wakefield asserted that his sister was still away with her mysterious friends and that he had yet to send off a message about the birth of his son. When pressed, he insisted that he could not until he heard from Lucy as they were traveling about and there was no way to reach her. But as soon as he heard from her, he would communicate Aubrey's eagerness to speak with her. Wakefield pledged Aubrey of this with a smirk that did not give him any real assurance of the man's good faith in the matter.

Brooding, he waited for someone to bring his horse out. Young Jack led out his gelding from the barn and held him while Aubrey mounted. In a low voice, he asked, "Did you talk to her, my lord? Before she left?"

Startled, Aubrey looked down. "Was Lady Lucilla here?"

The young man looked confused. "She arrived last evenin' as I told you and stayed the night. She left barely a half-hour ago on her mare. But it was after you arrived, so I thought you must have seen her."

Aubrey tightened his hands on the reins, and his horse sidled slightly causing Jack to jump back. Wakefield had lied to him! Aubrey wanted to go back to the house and bloody his nose, but it would not do.

"Which way did she go, lad?"

"Across the fields toward the northern road. She could have been headed towards Dodworth or Barnsley."

Aubrey passed the lad a coin and headed back to Lovell Abbey. He needed to pull out maps and look at the towns along that way. Barnsley was about an hour away on horseback and Dodworth was slightly closer, but there were other villages even nearer. Lucy had ridden alone which showed that she was not traveling very far. He was sure he was close and would find her soon.

BY THE MORNING, AUBREY had put together a planned route. He packed enough clothes to stay overnight in an inn if he needed to. Using Debrett's, Aubrey had identified manors and estates owned by families that might have taken Lucy in for a visit. He did not believe she would stay alone in an inn without a maid. Once she was sure it was safe, or she was over whatever had spooked her, Lucy would return to Wakefield Park and her family there. But he was sure he would find her before then.

By evening, he was not so sure. He had stopped at several places to inquire, but Aubrey had not thought out how people might react to a man asking about a single lady whose whereabouts was unknown. After stopping at Locke Park and being questioned severely by a stern older Baron, who had known his father, he had cobbled together a tale of assisting the Earl of Wakefield in finding his flighty sister who was visiting friends and was unaware of the birth of her new nephew. He thought it close enough to the truth that people might not question the veracity of the tale. Aubrey skipped over why a Viscount was the errand-boy for the Earl of Wakefield, and he had no answer as a groom or footman could serve in his place.

He rode up to the Salted Gull Inn in Dodworth, determined to stay the night. It was clean and his supper filling, if plain. The innkeeper was a rotund individual named Terrill, who responded with a laugh when Aubrey inquired as to the name of the place.

"My uncle originally owned the place. He had retired from the King's Navy and chose the name for reasons of his own. People around here know it well, so I kept it when my wife and I took it over."

Mr. Terrill could not help when Aubrey described Lucy and his search. He called out his wife, a sweaty woman with wisps of hair trailing from her topknot, from her place in the kitchen, but she did not recognize Lucy either.

"Dodworth is but a tiny place, my lord, and we don't get many of the nobs stayin' here. They go on to Barnsley."

Aubrey nodded, tired from his day in the saddle and unsure of his course. Barnsley seemed too big and too far away for Lucy to be found there. He had a feeling she would stay at a country estate not that far from Wakefield Park, not in a village or town.

"Course she could be over towards Oxspring or Crane Moor. You'd have to go a fair ways 'round as the roads don't hardly go that way, but it wouldn't be far from Wakefield cross-country as the crow flies. Someone who knows the old cart tracks could get about that ways." A grizzled older man sitting by the fire with his pint had overheard their conversation.

Terrill slapped his belly. "Why that's so, Samuel, so 'tis. Lovely country over there."

Something tickled Aubrey's memory, and he pulled out his map. There it was, Crane Moor, directly north of Wakefield Park if you cut across country. Lucy had mentioned something about it once, something to do with her father. He folded the map.

"Thank you, gentlemen, Mrs. Terrill. I believe you might have aided me more than you know." He threw coins on the table and sought his room. He could feel it, he had her now.

AUBREY WHISTLED TO himself as his horse picked his way down the overgrown path. He had been riding steadily since leaving Dodworth, and he thought he must be nearing Crane Moor. The day was sunny, and he was in a good mood, all because of an old man drinking his pint by the fire. When old Samuel had mentioned Crane Moor, Aubrey recognized it immediately. He could not remember why at first, just that it was significant. He had just about fallen asleep when it came to him. Crane Moor was where Lucy's father had bought a house for his mistress, the widow who was Lucy's mother.

It was just possible Lucy was staying there. Perhaps she had even inherited the house as part of her portion. Somehow Aubrey was confident he would find her there.

When he arrived, he found that Crane Moor was a tiny village, the church sitting at one end of the street and a public-house at the other end of the town. There were narrow rows of houses lining the way. He got down at the public-house and went in for a pint and some information.

The owner was glad to serve him the pint, but not the information. Mr. Rusby was a suspicious sort, one of those taciturn Northerners famous in the more garrulous South of England. No, no house had any young ladies staying in them. No, there were no young ladies of quality living in the village. There were only decent folks in Crane Moor, and young women were not encouraged to flit about on their own unaccounted for.

With each chary word and mistrustful look from the pub owner, Aubrey's heart sank. He must have been wrong or misremembered what Lucy had said. He thanked Rusby for the pint and went back out to his horse, trying to decide where to go next. Perhaps this was futile. The north of England was mostly country, and he could look for days and never find Lucy. Maybe it was better to wait her out. She had to come home to Wakefield Park, eventually.

Dejected, he rode his horse out of the village heading south. The road would go west for a short while, over the moors to Manchester, but he hoped to pick up another cart track he could follow home to Lovell Abbey. The sun had gone under a cloud as if to accommodate his new mood. He expected that he would run into a storm before he got home the way his luck was running.

His horse seemed to have picked up on his mood and plodded along, head down while Aubrey brooded. They came around a bend in the road to find a fair-sized home made of gray stone, a hedge across the front and outbuildings in the back. Flowers clustered around the door, brightening the yard as the sun came out from under the cloud. Aubrey drew on the reins and stopped his horse. His heart lightened as certainty grew within him.

After tying his horse to the gate in the center of the hedge, he rapped on the house door. There was no noise inside, so he knocked once more and heard footsteps coming to the doorway. The door swung open, and Lucy stood there, dressed with an apron over her morning gown, her hair falling messily down around her ears, and a smudge on one cheek. She had never looked so beautiful.

"Are you the maid?" Aubrey blurted out horrified, all his sangfroid gone. Had he driven her to this?

Lucy turned bright red and hurriedly pulled off the apron, bundling it up and leaving it on a nearby table. "Of course not. I was doing gardening in the back and came in to get a drink. What are you doing here?"

Aubrey regained some of his poise. "I am looking for you. May I please enter?"

For a minute, he thought she would refuse, but she stepped back and allowed him into the narrow hallway. "This way," she said as she led him into a cozy parlor. Lucy let him walk past her then pulled the door almost shut, carefully leaving it open enough to observe the proprieties.

The parlor was sunny and furnished with comfortable furniture, a room lived in. Needlework lay on a side table, and a book was open on the sofa. Lucy picked it up and moved it to the table, but remained standing. She thought this was to be a short interview. Aubrey walked to the nearby fireplace, china figurines dotting the mantel and turned to study her. She set her mouth with a mulish cast, and she kept looking nervously towards the doorway as if expecting another visitor.

Aubrey pulled his gloves off waiting for Lucy to explain herself.

"I thought you were Richard," she said. She realized her mistake when he swung his gloves at his thigh, connecting with a thwack.

"So he knows where you are."

"I asked him not to convey my whereabouts," she answered. "To anyone," she added as his eyes flashed.

"Why, Lucilla? Why did you leave and why not allow me to know where you were hiding?"

She winced. "I am not hiding. This is my home." She sank down onto the sofa, but Aubrey was too overwrought to seat himself.

Bewildered, he echoed, "Your home? Your home is Wakefield Park."

"No, this is my home. I have lived here for over five years. I visit the Park, and Richard comes here every week. Today is the day he usually arrives, but I thought he might not come today because of the new baby."

"You are a young lady of means and substance. You cannot live on your own. Do you have a chaperone?"

"Mary, my maid, is with me. That is adequate for...." She trailed off at Aubrey's look of dismay.

There was a clatter of footsteps in the hallway, and a woman's voice called out as the door to the parlor pushed open. A young girl raced into the room, her hands carefully cupping a bird's nest. Brown curls the same shade as Lucy's hair blew behind her as she ran to Lucy and plopped the nest in her lap. An older woman, puffing with her hand to her chest stopped in the doorway, her eyes wide as she saw Aubrey.

"Mama, look what we found on our walk!" the girl's childish treble trilled with excitement. "Mary said we could show you since the mama bird had taken her children away with her."

Lucy had paled, but she remained composed as she answered. "How nice, Annabelle." She smiled at the mess in her lap and then pushed the hair off the girl's forehead. "It is a lovely nest. You may put it on your window shelf if you would like."

"Do you think the mama bird will come back to it there if we leave the window open?"

Lucy laughed. "No, darling, I think the mama bird will find a new home, one that will not come down in a strong wind. Now go with Mary and take your treasure please as I have company."

The little girl spun, not having noticed Aubrey when she entered the room. Aubrey felt it as a physical blow when he looked into her face, so much like her mothers, but with his golden eyes.

Chapter Twenty-Five

The little girl took a few steps towards him, but stopped and looked back to her mother, suddenly uncertain. Aubrey swallowed hard and went down on his knee, smiling at the child.

"Hullo," she said, studying him carefully.

"Annabelle, make your curtsy to Lord Lovell please."

The child bit her lip and made a slight dip holding onto her skirts. She looked at her mother for approval and Lucy gave her a wavering smile, overwhelmed by a sight she had thought she would never see.

"What is your name?" Aubrey thought his heart would beat out of his chest.

"Annabelle," she replied with a frown.

"Of course, your mother just said so." Aubrey was not used to speaking with young children. He wanted to just drink her in, her perfect little face framed in her mother's curls. "How old are you, Annabelle?" Lucy started but did not say a word.

"I am four years old. Who are you, sir?"

Aubrey glanced at Lucy. "I am an old friend of your mother. We were neighbors once upon a time."

"You lived here?"

"No, near to your Uncle Richard. Your mama lived at Wakefield Park when she was a little girl like yourself."

"I am a big girl." Annabelle eyed him suspiciously. "Uncle Richard comes here to see us. He said I could come to visit him when I'm a big girl, but he says not yet. I have a new cousin, Ned."

"I had heard that." Aubrey wanted to touch the girl, his daughter, *his daughter*, but he did not want to startle or frighten her. "Your hair is very like your mama's curls, Annabelle." He savored the sound of her name. He had a daughter. Why had Lucy called her Annabelle? He was shaking, so he stood again, trying to regain control of his limbs and he put one hand on the mantel to steady himself.

The maid, governess, whatever she was, came forward. "Annabelle, we must put your nest away. Come with me now, and we will see if Cook has treats and a cold drink after our walk." Lucy handed the woman the pile of twigs and straw that Annabelle had left in her lap and Annabelle quietly followed her out of the room. When she reached the door, she turned and gave another of her dips, placing her foot in front of her to balance.

"Mama. Lord..." she scrunched up her nose trying to remember.

'*Papa, you can call me Papa,*' Aubrey thought, but he did not dare to voice his thoughts. "Lord Lovell, Annabelle. And it was very nice to meet you." She smiled and ran after her nurse.

Aubrey watched her go, feeling a hole open in his heart as she disappeared. He had a daughter, and he had missed almost five years of her life. He had not even known of her existence. How could Lucy have not told him? He felt cold as he turned to her. She sat on the sofa still, her face strained and hands clasped together so tightly that they showed white against her brown dress.

"She is my daughter." He said it flatly, cruelly, and she flinched and bowed her head. "How could you not tell me?"

Lucy took a deep breath, trying to gird herself for the confrontation and looked up. "You were long gone by the time I knew I was with child. I was left abandoned and ruined. I was lucky that my family stood by me and continued to aid me."

"And when I returned? Could you not have told me then?"

"Things were strained between us at first. Once we were..." Lucy blushed, "friends again I tried to speak to you, but never had a good opportunity. When I heard you were to marry, I knew I could never tell you. You would want Annabelle, and I would not have her raised by another woman, not one that might be cruel to her, who might not love her. My family sacrificed much to allow me to keep her, and I will not give up my daughter."

Aubrey shook his head, much of his anger cooling as her words penetrated through the haze of outrage. He walked across the room to sink down next to her on the sofa and took her hands in his.

"Lucy, I am marrying you, not some other woman. I thought you understood that. You are mine. I love you, and now I love our daughter. We are meant to be together forever if you will have me."

Lucy stared at him wildly, and a tear trickled down her cheek. She inhaled, and an intense storm of tears broke forth. Aubrey pulled her close and let her cry until the tears permeated his broadcloth coat and he could feel the linen of his shirt becoming damp.

"Damn you, damn you." The storm was passing, and Lucy vainly wiped at her face until Aubrey pulled out a handkerchief and handed it to her. She blew her nose and lifted tired eyes to him.

"Please do not take Annabelle from me."

Aubrey pulled her onto his lap and settled her head against his chest.

"Lucy, love, did you hear me? I love you, I love Annabelle, and I intend to marry you, and we shall be a family."

She struggled to sit up so she could see his face. "But what about Lady Clarissa? You are to marry her. And I cannot let her raise Annabelle."

"Lucy, please calm down and listen. I will never marry Lady Clarissa or anyone else but you. Tell me you understand what I am saying to you?"

She blinked her eyes and shook her head. "Wait, you want to marry me? I thought at one time perhaps, but your mother and Lady Clarissa said you meant to have me as your mistress. I could not do that to Annabelle or my family, no matter how much I love you."

"You love me?" Aubrey filed away the information about his mother and her acolyte but focused on the one bit that was important.

"Of course."

"And you will marry me? Say yes, Lucy, I need to hear it from your lips. I have a special license, and we can be married as soon as we can arrange it."

"Yes, yes."

Aubrey crushed his lips to hers and held her close. There were more matters they had to clear up, but for now, he needed to kiss her. She was frantic trying to pull him closer, her small hands entwined in his hair as she met his tongue with her own. Lucy moaned, overcome by a sudden passion until....

"Mama." They broke apart to find Annabelle looking at them with confusion in her golden eyes. "What are you doing?"

Lucy jumped off of Aubrey's lap and poked at her hair, pushing stray tendrils back into place. Meanwhile, Aubrey stood up and walked several steps away, his back to them while he calmed his errant body.

"Lord Lovell and I were talking." Annabelle wrinkled her nose, looking back and forth between them. "Did you need me for something? Where is Mary?"

Annabelle was successfully distracted and looked guiltily over her shoulder at the doorway. "I wanted to show you how the nest looks on my shelf. Mary went to get our luncheon."

Lucy took her daughter's hand and led her to the hallway. "You must not run away from Mary. She is probably looking for you. Go back up to the nursery, and I will speak to you later."

The little girl pouted, but walked up the stairs, holding onto the railing. Lucy watched until she had reached the top and disappeared toward her room. Then she smoothed her skirts and turned back to the parlor.

Aubrey grinned ruefully as she came back in the room. "I think it will take an adjustment, this becoming a father so suddenly."

Feeling shy, Lucy stood behind a chair as if to use it as a shield. "We need to talk."

"Yes," he agreed. "We *do* need to talk." He motioned for her to take the chair and she sat while he moved to the sofa. For this discussion, it was needful to have a space between them.

"Tell me what happened after you found you were with child. I would like to hear the entire story," Aubrey said.

Lucy twisted her hands together and looked down at the floor. No one had heard this whole story, not even her family. She began in a quiet voice, so Aubrey had to strain to hear her, but it gradually grew stronger.

"After you left for Italy, I went into a decline. I could not understand why you had gone when I thought we would be planning our marriage. I slept all the time and did not eat. My parents thought I had caught a summer fever, and a doctor was called, but he found naught the matter with me. My mother realized that I was with child. I did not understand."

Lucy looked up. "My parents were all that was kind. I never told them who the father was, but I believe they knew. Richard was away in London, but he came home to help. Before anyone else realized that I was carrying a child, my mother and I moved here. My father had kept the house after my birth mother died and had been renting it out. He moved the tenants out, so we had a place to stay. Annabelle was born here."

"My family had put about that I was a widow. My young husband had gone to Europe on business and died there from a fever. Of course, the village people knew who my parents were, and I suspect many thought the tale untrue, but they have been kind over the years. It helped that my family did not repudiate me. I am known as Mrs. Sutcliffe here."

Aubrey raised an eyebrow in question, and Lucy huffed out a reply. "Richard went to school with a Sutcliffe. The man had a lung disease and went to Europe for a cure. Richard appropriated his last name though we have never given my fake husband a first name."

Lucy was relaxing a little. "Annabelle and I have lived here ever since. Occasionally, I visit Wakefield Park, but I have never brought Annabelle there. Too many people would question her existence. But she has become old enough to ask questions and to want to know more."

She stood and walked to the fireplace, too restless to sit, and Aubrey automatically stood with her, watching her as she paced. "Richard wanted to adopt Annabelle and raise her as his own. He thought he would give me the chance to have a season and find a husband. So I tried for his sake, but I would not give her up, and I could imagine none of the men I met as her father."

Aubrey walked over and took her hands. "Can you imagine me in that role?"

Both their hands trembled with emotion, and the tears trickled down Lucy's cheeks once more. He wiped the tears away with his thumb and kissed her forehead.

"There is no one else, it has always been you," she whispered.

Chapter Twenty-Six

After they had spent their emotions, Lucy and Aubrey retired to the small dining room for luncheon. Lucy had a village woman who came in to cook for lunch and dinner and two other women who came twice a week to do the cleaning and laundry. Aside from a groom who cared for their horses and Mary, her onetime maid who now acted as a nurse for Annabelle, there was no one else in the house.

They continued to talk and plan, excited and ready to move on to the next phase of their lives. Lucy was finally convinced of Aubrey's devotion. His pride in his newfound daughter made her additionally happy. For many years, she was sure it would not please him to learn that he had fathered a child, but his joy was clear. He wanted to know every little thing about Annabelle.

She convinced him they should wait for a time, not marry right away, and allow Annabelle to become familiar with Aubrey. Lucy and Annabelle would move back to Wakefield Park where Aubrey could visit every day. When they judged the time to be right, they would tell their child that Aubrey was her father and that they were marrying.

Aubrey wanted to use the special license immediately and bring his family to Lovell Abbey, but he deferred to Lucy and the needs of his daughter.

"Not over two weeks, Lucy," he warned her. "I cannot wait more than that to have you as my wife. It seems as if I have been waiting forever."

"I will be ready," she promised. "I only need Richard and Anne to bear witness."

"Would you not like a wedding like Harriet and George had? All the people and fuss?" he teased.

"No, never. Just you and my brother and his wife. Oh, and, of course, Annabelle. We cannot tell her until the last minute, or she will make herself ill with excitement."

"Do you think she will like me?"

"Oh, Aubrey." Lucy stood up from the table and came to sit on his lap. She put her arms around his neck. "Of course, she will love you. You are her father."

"I loved my father, Lucy, but I did not like him much."

"You will play with her and spoil her, and I will be the disciplinarian that both of you will disobey." Lucy smiled. "Just wait until she is overtired and has a tantrum. I will depend on you to soothe her."

Aubrey chuckled, but he was nervous. His own parents had not set much of an example for him to follow, but he was determined to establish a new course. And Lucy would be by his side to help him.

"I must pack a few things for Annabelle and myself, at least for a few days. I will leave Mary to do the rest, and I can send Richard's carriage back for her and the luggage." She hopped off of his lap. "I hope that Richard will allow us to stay for a short time."

"Of course, he will. You told me he has wanted you both there for ages. But I will send back a carriage for Mary and your things, no need for him to do so."

They had agreed to ride to Wakefield Park once they had made all arrangements. By carriage, it was several hours, and Lucy did not want to wait now they had settled on a plan. Lucy went to speak to Mary and Cook while Aubrey waited in the parlor, trying to calm his nerves.

"Oh, you are still here." Annabelle had escaped from Mary again. He wondered how common an occurrence this was. Then he wondered how much he could tell her without incurring Lucy's wrath.

"Yes, I am waiting for you and your mother. I am escorting you on a journey this afternoon."

Annabelle thought this over. "Where are we going?" she asked flatly.

Aubrey smiled pleasantly. "That is up to your mother to tell you."

She looked towards the stairs, apparently torn between running to ask her mama and trying to see if she might get more information out of him.

"Did you know my Papa?"

Aubrey felt a trickle of sweat go down his back. "Yes."

"Can you tell me about him? It makes mama sad when I ask about him." She was so earnest that Aubrey wanted to hug her to him and reassure her he would never let her go, but he restrained himself.

"I think your mama will tell you more about your Papa shortly." Annabelle nodded and turned to go. "But Annabelle, know this. He loves you very much."

She stared at him thoughtfully, gave a short nod and left to find her mother. A few moments later Aubrey heard shrieks. Lucy must have told her where they were journeying. He smiled to himself. His life was about to become quite lively.

LUCY HAD WARNED AUBREY that Annabelle usually took a nap in the afternoon. Since he had her up in front of him on his horse, he expected that she might nod off at some point. But she was so excited to be on a horse she wiggled and turned, trying to see everything at once. He had to caution her when they started out, and he reminded her once again before Lucy spoke to her more firmly, and Annabelle settled down.

As the ride wore on, she slumped back against Aubrey, tired but not willing to miss anything. He relished the small warm body cuddled against him and did his best to answer her questions about her surroundings. Lucy rode next to them, a gentle smile on her lips and allowed Aubrey to deal with her mostly.

By the time they rode through the gates of Wakefield Park Annabelle was blinking and yawning. She revived as they reached the front of the house and her eyes grew big when a footman came out to assist Lucy down from her horse. Aubrey swung down and lifted Annabelle, setting her on the gravel carriageway.

"Uncle Richard," Annabelle squealed. Richard had come out to see who had arrived. He took his niece and swung her up into his arms with an ease that Aubrey envied. Richard gave Aubrey a sharp look before he turned to his sister to greet her.

"Richard, we have much to share with you, but first may we impose on you for a few days?" Lucy asked. She could not help wringing her hands slightly, and Aubrey moved to stand by her for support.

"What do you think, Annabelle? Should we allow your mother to stay or do I get to have you to myself?" Richard was teasing, and Aubrey eased as Lucy relaxed, the tension leaving her body.

"I want my mama," Annabelle said with a quaver.

"Then you shall have her. Come in, come in and meet your new cousin. Your Aunt Anne had just brought him downstairs for a visit when we saw you ride up." Richard led them into the house while the footman handed over their reins to Jack, who had come at a run from the stables. The cheeky lad winked at Aubrey as he took their horses off to care for them.

Once they were inside, there was the predictable cooing over the new baby. Annabelle was in awe, gently patting a leg where the child lay on Anne's lap. Aubrey felt an unexpected tightening in his chest. He had missed the first few years of Annabelle's life. He regretted that deeply now. Aubrey would never see her as Ned looked now, and he fiercely vowed not to pass over any more opportunities to take part in her life.

Anne was patently delighted at their news, whispered discreetly to her by Lucy. Richard was more discreet in his satisfaction at his sister's clear happiness. When he offered Aubrey a brandy, he clinked his glass with a nod of approval.

"I assume you have worked out your issues with my sister," he murmured.

Aubrey smiled. If you and I are soon to be brothers by marriage means that Lucy and I agree, then you are correct. But Annabelle does not know yet. We want to let her become accustomed to the idea first which is why we are imposing upon your hospitality."

"I have wanted them both here for quite some time, but could not convince Lucy so them staying here is not an issue. We need to have a discussion about Annabelle. Some years ago I inquired about legitimizing her birth status. I did not have the authority but based on what they told me, I believe you may take steps in that direction."

Aubrey felt a weight lift off his shoulders he did not even realize was there. "I confess, I only found about her existence this morning, but I have every intention of writing to my solicitor for advice as soon as I am able. I would appreciate any insight you might have."

Richard grinned. "It may require a bit of subterfuge and influence, but I have every confidence we can find a solution, especially if we keep your wedding somewhat quiet. I assume that is the plan. I know my sister, and an assembly would appall her at her nuptials."

"Absolutely. I already have a special license for when she's ready. I would be honored if you would stand for me and I believe Lucy is asking Anne. That is all we need for witnesses."

"And your daughter will insist on attending, I'm sure."

Aubrey glanced over to where Annabelle had fallen asleep on the sofa, head in her mother's lap. "I should carry her up to bed, and then I must ride back to Lovell Abbey. I will also send to my solicitor regarding the settlements, but you will find no impediment on my side. Anything that Lucy and Annabelle require shall be theirs."

"I expected no less," Richard answered.

Aubrey walked over to the sofa and lifted his sleeping daughter. "Lead the way," he whispered to Lucy, and she rose to show him to the nursery which Annabelle would share with Ned for the night. Lucy undressed her sleepy child and got her ready for bed. Aubrey kissed her cheek. But Annabelle was already asleep, tired out from her exciting day. He put his arms around Lucy and pulled her close.

"I must be away, but I will return in the morning. Perhaps we can take Annabelle on a picnic if the day is fine."

"She would like that," Lucy smoothed his cravat. "I can speak to Cook, I am sure that Richard would not mind."

"Richard is euphoric with our circumstances and cannot wait for them to be finalized on our wedding day." He kissed her forehead although he wanted more. "I cannot wait myself."

Lucy walked him downstairs, not wanting to let him go but knowing he had much to settle. He knew she was tired also, so he called for his horse and rode home in the gathering dusk, his heart light and mind busy with the actions he must take in the next few days. He would need to meet with the local clergyman, send a coach for Lucy's things, and start preparations for a new mistress at Lovell Abbey.

Therefore, he was not prepared to find unexpected visitors when he walked into the house and discovered both his mother and Lord Rathburn in residence. They had arrived earlier in the day, and his mother was waiting for him impatiently.

"Lovell, it is past time for you to be home. Where have you been?"

Aubrey ignored her question. "Mother, I did not expect you here. And Rathburn, I especially did not expect you." He glared at the man with dislike.

"What would you have me do when you left Blakesley's wedding so abruptly? I needed an escort, and Lord Rathburn kindly agreed to my request." His mother tipped her chin in the air, displaying her disdain.

"I would have expected you to return to your sister's house in London rather than make the trek to Yorkshire when you dislike the country so much." Aubrey was pointed in his rejoinder.

"It is incumbent on me to not allow you to make any rash decisions. I decided that you might need my advice." His mother had a false smile and too sweet tone. She never could dissemble successfully. He ignored her for the moment and concentrate on her escort.

"Well, Rathburn, I thank you for accompanying my mother on her journey, but you need not stay longer than tonight. I am sure you, at least, are eager to return to the delights of London." Aubrey gave the older man a steely glare that Rathburn seemed to ignore.

"A repairing lease in the country is just what I need right now. Your esteemed mother has extended her hospitality, and I am glad to take advantage."

"My mother does not have the right to invite guests to my home." Aubrey decided that plain-speaking was in order. "I will be glad to make a carriage available to take you wherever you might wish to go."

"Do not be ridiculous, Lovell. Lord Rathburn is my guest." His mother's neck was turning red, a sure sign of her agitation.

"And this is my home now, mother. I would suggest that you take advantage of Lord Rathburn's escort once more when he leaves."

Aubrey turned to leave but stopped when Rathburn spoke once more. "I suppose that you were at Wakefield Park visiting the lovely Lady Lucilla."

He spun back around. "Stay away from Lady Lucilla."

Rathburn exchanged glances with Lady Lovell, picking at the cuff of his jacket. "But Lady Lucilla and I are old friends. I would like to pay her a visit while I am here."

Aubrey wanted to bloody the man's nose. It seemed as if he would have to have him thrown out bodily. And his mother as well. But that would cause a scandal he wanted to avoid at this point. He heaved in a deep breath.

"They are not receiving visitors at Wakefield Park at present. The Countess has just presented the Earl with an heir."

Rathburn smirked. "But you said you had just come from there?"

"I am treated like family as I grew up nearby. I do not believe you can claim my type of acquaintance. Now if you will excuse me, I have matters to attend to. I will take a dinner tray in my office."

Aubrey left the room, but he was uneasy. His mother was up to no good and Rathburn was a cad who was using her to his own advantage. He must keep them away from Wakefield Park and remove them from Lovell Abbey as soon as possible.

Chapter Twenty-Seven

The next day dawned bright and clear. Lucy had fallen into a deep sleep the night before but was up early to check on Annabelle. Her daughter was usually up first, and she might be uneasy in her new surroundings. Lucy found Annabelle sitting with Ned's nurse having a breakfast of bread with honey and milk. She appeared to have settled in well, not at all bothered by waking up in a strange bed. And Clara, Ned's nurse, was a kindly woman used to small children, so she had made Annabelle comfortable.

Watching her daughter chatter to Clara, Lucy reflected that Annabelle would adapt to having a father and a new family situation quite well. She would also be happy with the proximity between Wakefield Park and Lovell Abbey. Annabelle knew her aunt and uncle well and missed them when they could not visit. Perhaps it was not too soon to sit her daughter down and reveal that she had a loving father whom they would reside with soon.

"Annabelle, we are to have a special picnic today with Lord Lovell. Would you enjoy that?"

A squeal of delight was her answer, and Lucy looked nervously to the next room where Ned was still sleeping. Clara went to check on her primary charge, so Lucy took advantage of the privacy.

"Do you like Lord Lovell, Annabelle?"

Annabelle looked up with milk dripping from the corner of her mouth. Lucy wiped at her face with a napkin and waited.

"Yes, Mama, I do."

"I know that you just met him, but he is nice, don't you think?"

"Yes, Mama." Annabelle seemed more interested in the last drops of honey on her plate. Lucy bit back a sigh. Children, she found, were pragmatic mostly and accepted new situations and people with ease. She would have to keep her fingers crossed that Annabelle followed that pattern card.

"I will dress and have my breakfast. I will come up and get you when Lord Lovell arrives."

Annabelle nodded and submitted to Clara's wiping off her sticky hands and face. "I will get her dressed and ready, my lady," Clara said.

By the time Aubrey arrived Lucy was pacing the hallway. He laughed and took her hands.

"So eager to see me, my love?"

She calmed at his touch. "I thought yesterday was all a dream."

"A happy dream that will continue for the rest of our lives. Although I have a fly in our ointment. Or rather two of the same ilk."

"What is it?" Lucy was nervous.

"My mother has arrived at Lovell Abbey and has also brought Lord Rathburn."

"Rathburn!" Lucy grew pale at the words. "Why in the world would she bring him?"

"I suspect to discommode the both of us. I put a flea in both their ears, asked them to leave, but I fear being too forceful as I do not want to create the opportunity for any more scenes."

Aubrey put the back of a gloved hand on her cheek, regardless of the footman nearby. "Do not bother your pretty head, my love. I suspect that they will go in a day or two, especially if I am spending much of my time here. They already know they aren't invited to Wakefield Park."

"If you say so I will not concern myself." Lucy did not look relieved, but Aubrey was happy that she would leave it to him.

"How is Annabelle this morning?"

"She is excited about our picnic." Lucy pulled her hands away to clasp them at her waist. "She is adjusting well to all the changes in her life. I think she will be ready for more alterations soon."

"The sooner she is the better I like it," Aubrey said with a grin. "Where is she anyway?"

"Let me get her." Lucy turned to the footman. "James, would you please retrieve the basket I asked Cook to prepare for our picnic? Thank you."

Once Lucy had brought Annabelle downstairs, Aubrey took the basket on one arm and Annabelle's hand in the other. Lucy had her daughter's other hand as they walked across the broad lawn to the pond set off near the woods. Aubrey spread the blanket at the top of the basket and Lucy laid out the food that Cook had packed for them. Annabelle kept up a steady chatter, her parents responding to her myriad questions and laughing just from the enjoyment of the day and being with each other.

When they finished with their meal, Lucy wrapped up the remainders and stored it in the basket.

"Shall we take a walk around the pond and see if some exercise revives us after that delicious and filling meal?" Aubrey asked.

Annabelle's face turned to her mother, pleading for her assent, and Lucy laughed. "I agree as long as we take a nap upon our return." When her daughter pouted, Lucy added, "We will sleep outside here under the shade of these trees, Annabelle." The child jumped up and down in excitement and Lucy looked at Aubrey to see if he agreed.

"I think we would find that refreshing." He waggled his eyebrows at her. Lucy gave him a quelling look but shook her head in amusement. They started off, Lucy on Aubrey's arm while Annabelle ran back and forth, gathering posies, rocks, or anything else she found of interest. She would bring them back to show her parents and Aubrey found that his pockets became the repository for many of her finds.

"You know, you don't have to keep everything she finds," Lucy said to him in a low voice.

"I suppose so, but I feel as if I have missed so much that everything is important now."

Lucy laughed. "That will pass with time, at least to a degree. You will decide what is the most precious and keep those items."

"I already know what is most valuable and I intend to keep this forever," Aubrey replied solemnly. He put his arm around her waist, and Lucy felt like the luckiest woman in the world. They walked for a while on the path around the pond, keeping an eye on Annabelle, so she did not go too close to the water. Lucy expected that her boots and stockings would be damp, but she was thankful that Annabelle had not yet pulled them off to run barefoot through the grass.

Lucy was relaxed and truly happy. It was a beautiful day, and all was right in her world for once. So she was not prepared when Rathburn stepped out of the woods to confront Annabelle. The girl stopped dead and looked back at her parents when Rathburn addressed her. Lucy could not hear what he said, but both she and Aubrey picked up speed to reach their daughter.

"Lady Lucilla, Lord Lovell, what a pleasant day for a stroll." His teeth gleamed as he simpered and gave a bow.

"Annabelle, come here please," Lucy ordered. Aubrey did not wait for her response, but strode forward and picked the child up in his arms.

"Rathburn, what are you doing here? I told you that Wakefield Park was out of bounds for you." Aubrey was trying to stay calm in front of his daughter but was finding it difficult to restrain himself. "You should be packing your things and aiding my mother in preparations for leaving Yorkshire."

"Oh, did I leave the bounds of Lovell Abbey? I did not notice. But how lovely to see this happy family group."

Lucy's pulse was hammering, and she wanted to take Annabelle and run away from this horrid man. Annabelle appeared comfortable in Aubrey's arms, but she was listening avidly. Lucy was not sure if she understood what was being said, but she did not want it laid out any plainer.

"Aubrey, you can deal with your guest. Annabelle and I will walk back to the Park." He nodded and put Annabelle down, then Lucy quickly took her hand, and they walked back the way they had come. She felt prickles on her back, knowing Rathburn was watching them depart, all the while planning feverishly for ways to turn this to his advantage.

"Who was that man, mama?" Annabelle's face was grave as she walked with no protest to where they had had the picnic.

"He is not a nice man. He is temporarily staying at Lovell Moor with your Gran.., Lord Lovell's mother, as her guest." Heavens, Lucy was flustered. She had almost said grandmother. But Annabelle did not appear to notice her slip.

"Will Lord Lovell be safe by himself?"

Lucy's heart overflowed, and tears burned in her eyes. "I am sure he will be fine. He knows how to deal with bad people, and he will always protect us, sweetheart."

Annabelle said nothing more and didn't protest when Lucy bypassed the picnic blanket and basket to return to the house. Lucy turned her over to Clara for her nap and went back down to wait for Aubrey. The house was quiet. Anne was resting, and Richard was out on the estate.

She flew to the doorway when Aubrey came in carrying the picnic basket from their interrupted afternoon.

"What did he say?" Lucy was pale and trembling but waited as James took the basket from Aubrey and disappeared.

"Not much," Aubrey replied grimly. "He asked questions about Annabelle, but I fended them off. I suspect he knows the truth however or, at the least, can make an accurate guess. I think I should ride home and ensure that both he and my mother are sent packing."

"But what if he tells someone?"

"It matters no longer, love. Richard and I can manage any fallout locally, and we will marry long before he can spread the news anywhere else. I was planning to put about that we had been secretly married before I left for Italy anyhow. As we intend to live quietly here in the north, for the most part, news such as this will be quickly forgotten."

Lucy gradually stopped shaking, his warm arm around her a comfort. She could not wait until they were finally married. He was right, they could manage this and Rathburn was not highly thought of by the Ton, anyway. Had she not already faced him down once? They could deal with this.

Aubrey gave her a quick kiss and headed to the stables for his horse. Lucy tried to settle with some needlework, but it was no use. She dearly wished that Anne was available, but she was nursing her new baby and needed to rest when she could.

A short time later there was a knock on the door, and Clara stood there with a concerned look on her face.

"Pardon me, my lady, but is the young miss here with you? I slipped out for just a moment to check on the baby, and when I came back, her cot was empty."

Lucy panicked. Could Rathburn have got access to the house and taken her? No, it was more likely that Annabelle was wandering. Back in Crane Moor, Annabelle had often slipped away from Mary, but never far or for long. She must be up to her old tricks.

"I have not seen her. Can you please ask the footmen to search the house? I will look also, but I don't want to disturb the Countess. You should go back to watch over the baby, Clara." She took a deep breath. "I am sure we will find her. Do not worry. She is just curious about the house."

It was not long before the house was searched and maids and footmen spread out across the estate to check the grounds. A groom was sent to Richard to call him home, and Anne was roused by the noise and was helping to look along with Lucy. No one had found Annabelle yet, and Lucy was more than worried. Another groom was sent to Aubrey to give him the news and ask for help from the people at Lovell Abbey.

Anne was coordinating the search from the front parlor while Lucy paced. One maid came into the room with a tea tray as Anne was going over a map from the estate office with the head stable master. The maid brought the tray over to Lucy, who motioned to take it away. Before she did, she slipped a paper into Lucy's hand. She shook her head to prevent any outcry and then moved away leaving the tea tray on a side table.

Lucy swiftly walked to the window so that her back was to the room and opened the note. When she had finished reading, she slipped away.

Chapter Twenty-Eight

Aubrey rode up to the house at a gallop. The groom had caught him out on some estate business, and he cursed the delay. When he had arrived home after the picnic, his mother had been resting, and Rathburn was nowhere to be found. He had tried to catch up on business affairs.

Richard had just mounted his own horse, and he spoke to Aubrey. The yard was a whirl of activity as tenants, servants, and neighbors shouted, and grooms managed horses and carriages.

"No one has not found yet. I have people looking everywhere, and I have just sent men down to the pond to look for her." Richard looked grim. "I have not given up. I think we will still find her safely."

Aubrey did not believe he could breathe from the pain clutching at his chest. "Where is Lucy?" he gasped.

"No one knows. She slipped out a short while ago. I hope that she has an inkling of where Annabelle may be."

Aubrey nodded. Lucy knew her daughter best. "What do you need me to do?"

"I am riding towards the eastern part of the estate. Perhaps you could try the border of your lands. Perhaps she headed towards Lovell Abbey."

Aubrey nodded and spun his horse back in the direction he had come. He thought about the men dredging the pond and shuddered. He had just found his daughter. Aubrey could not lose her now.

He rode back by the forest path around the water where they had walked earlier in the day. Perhaps Annabelle had noticed something, a treasure, and returned to find it later. Aubrey had carefully emptied his pockets once he reached home, saving her findings to give to her tomorrow. Please let him discover her to restore them to her.

His horse plunged under the branches of trees, and he slowed, avoiding the lower-hanging limbs. This was not a path typically used for riding, but it cut off towards Lovell Abbey. He and Lucy had often used it in their youth. Just over the boundary line was a folly that his father had erected. He and Lucy had met there, a place they could call their own. Instinct he couldn't countermand urged Aubrey towards it.

Just before he broke out of the woods onto his own land, he heard a shriek and a man shouting. Aubrey stopped and slid off his horse, tying it to a nearby branch. He crept forward towards the folly, careful not to make any noise. There was definitely a man and a woman talking, and he recognized Lucy's voice, high and frantic.

"The brat bit me. I should bloody her mouth for that." It was Rathburn. He had his back to Aubrey and was holding Annabelle.

"She does not know you, and you frightened her. She is just a little girl," Lucy pleaded. "Please let her go."

"I will let her go when you agree to come with me to Scotland. I need a wealthy bride, and you will do."

"Never will I marry you. Find another rich woman and let Annabelle go." Lucy caught sight of Aubrey creeping up behind Rathburn but did not change her expression.

"But do you not see? You are perfect for me. I only want your money and perhaps to bed you once or twice. Then you can go back to your bastard daughter and hide forever in the country. But my creditors are importuning me now, and I cannot wait any longer. Also, I will receive an incentive from Lady Lovell if I take you out of the running from marrying her idiot son."

"Her idiot son is standing right behind you," Aubrey said. Rathburn swung around as Lucy leaped forward and tore Annabelle from his grasp. Then Aubrey punched him in the face, knocking him to the ground.

"You bastard! I'll kill you," Aubrey growled as he pulled Rathburn back up and hit him again. "How dare you touch my daughter?"

Rathburn stumbled but did not fall again. Still, he was the worst for wear. He tried to land a blow at Aubrey, but Aubrey moved out of the way and hit him twice more, two swift jabs and Rathburn was knocked out cold.

Annabelle had stopped crying and was watching him wide-eyed as Lucy gathered her tightly in her arms.

"Lucy, take my horse, it's over under the trees, and return Annabelle to the house. Send men back here please and I will watch him until they get here. I want him locked up, and a magistrate called." Aubrey was panting, but he had hardly spoiled his toilette in the fight. Rathburn had not landed a blow.

Lucy nodded and ran with Annabelle, disappearing into the woods. In a moment, Aubrey heard the horse's hoofs beating away, and he sat on the steps of the folly, keeping an eye on his fallen foe.

Eventually, Rathburn regained consciousness. He groaned and sat up, holding his jaw. One eye was already swelling up, and his lip bled, staining his disheveled cravat. He pulled out an end and tenderly patted at his face with the least dirty place he could find. Aubrey watched scornfully as the rogue tried to put himself back together.

"Was it essential to hit me so many times?" Rathburn whined.

"If you had stayed conscious, I would have hit you more. You deserved it all and more." Aubrey sneered at Rathburn. "Stay where you are. There are men on their way to take you to the magistrate. Attempted kidnapping is a serious offense."

"Oh, I don't think you will have me arrested. If you do, I would have to expose Lady Lovell as part of the scheme." Rathburn was trying to be smug, but he looked ridiculous with his swollen lip and a black eye.

Aubrey laughed. "What makes you think I would care if it involved my mother? And as devious as she is, I do not believe she would be part of a kidnapping scheme. She brought you here to devise a way for you to force Lucy into marriage, but she would not dirty herself with the details. No one will believe you."

Rathburn paled. "But the scandal! Surely you don't want your daughter's name bandied about?"

"We'll see what the magistrate says," Aubrey replied, but Rathburn was right. Aubrey would never have Annabelle and Lucy's names besmirched as they would be if Rathburn were brought to justice.

Richard rode up at that moment accompanied by several men. His face was grim as he swung down from his mount.

"Lucy told me in brief what happened here. My men will take him back to the Park, and we can decide what to do then."

"We should call the magistrate," Aubrey said although he was far from sure that should be the case.

"Did you forget? I am the local magistrate," Richard replied with one eyebrow lifted. "I am judge and jury as far as Lord Rathburn is concerned. Perhaps he should have thought of that before he kidnapped my niece and importuned my sister." He nodded, and the men stepped forward and secured Rathburn's arms. He had no hope of freeing himself anyway, so he walked off with the men towards the Park.

"Are you all right? Lucy said it was quite the one-sided fight."

"I have not lost all my skills, and he was not much of an opponent." Aubrey hesitated, but said, "Do you think it wise to arraign Rathburn? He certainly deserves to be punished, but I worry over the consequences towards Annabelle and Lucy if this becomes more public."

"I thought of that. My people are trustworthy. They would not gossip beyond the locals." The two men walked back towards the estate, Richard leading his horse.

"Lucy thought that Rathburn desperately needs money. His creditors are after him, and he thought by taking Annabelle that he could force Lucy to marry him."

"Apparently he had encouragement from my mother. I will deal with her later."

Richard gave Aubrey a look of commiseration but did not respond, feeling it was a matter that Aubrey could attend to best. "I thought a solution for Rathburn might be to send him out of England. He would avoid his creditors, and if we ensured his cooperation in not being sent to gaol, then he would remain quiet about all aspects of this affair."

Aubrey blew out a sigh of relief. "If he agrees, I feel it would be the best possible solution."

"Oh, he will agree. I will ensure that he does."

Chapter Twenty-Nine

Aubrey and Richard came into Anne's private parlor where the women and Annabelle were sitting. They had thanked the servants and others who had helped with the search already, and Richard ordered a round of cider and beer for the thirsty helpers. Richard had also ensured that Rathburn was securely locked in the cellar. He had decided that leaving the man overnight to cool his heels might make him more amenable in the morning.

Aubrey went straight to Lucy and Annabelle, who was curled up next to her mother on a sofa.

"Annabelle, sweetheart, are you all right?" He took her small hands in his gloved hands, peering into her face.

"Papa, I have a boo here." She held up her arm to show him a bruise from where Rathburn had grabbed her. He wanted to punch the man once more until he realized what she had said. He marked Lucy, who was smiling and had tears in her eyes.

"Annabelle, I will let no one ever hurt you again." He gathered her close, and her arms went around his neck.

"And Annabelle will never wander off on her own again, will she?" Lucy remonstrated when Aubrey had pulled back.

"No, Mama. I wanted to see my Grandmamma." Annabelle wiggled around to look up at her mother. "I never had a Grandmamma, and I wanted to see where she lives with Papa."

Aubrey did not know what to say. He swallowed hard and quirked an eyebrow in question at Lucy.

"Annabelle determined that you were her Papa. She heard me say something about your mother living at Lovell Abbey for the time being. She has a habit of listening to adults talking when she should not."

"Are you happy that I am your Papa, Annabelle?" Aubrey was nervous, but he found that little girls are far more practical than he knew.

"Yes, Papa." She looked at him in disbelief. "You know good Papas give their daughters a pony of their very own." She smiled as the adults laughed.

"We must see what your mama has to say to that, sweetheart. And I have to see what the stables at Lovell Abbey have in the way of ponies."

"But how will I see him if he lives in your stables?"

Aubrey glanced at Lucy, and she nodded in encouragement.

"Perhaps if you and your Mama came to live at Lovell Abbey with me you could see him every day?"

Annabelle clapped her hands. "Oh, yes, and with my Grandmamma, too!"

"Grandmama may go on an extended visit for the time being," Aubrey responded dryly. "But I expect that you will meet many new people. Do not forget that you will be neighbors to your aunt and uncle and new cousin."

"Well, Ned is not much fun yet. I'm ready to go." She slid off of her mother's lap and started for the door.

"Wait a moment," Richard caught up to his niece and swung her up in the air. "Are you bored with Aunt Anne and me too?"

Annabelle squealed with delight as her uncle tossed her a little higher, then lowered her to the floor. "Again, again."

"You are getting too big for me to lift you that high. Perhaps you should go live at Lovell Abbey, and your papa can play with you." Richard winked. "But you must come to visit the Park often, now you know the way here."

Aubrey sat next to Lucy and took her hand. He whispered, "She seems fine with a new Papa and house. Is it truly so?"

Lucy squeezed his hand. "Yes, she is happy. As am I." She blushed and bit her lip. "I believe we could move ahead with our wedding plans. There seems to be no further impediment."

"Thank God! Would the day after tomorrow be too soon?"

Lucy smiled in agreement, and Aubrey lifted her hands and impressed a quick kiss on her knuckles. "Then after we deal with Rathburn tomorrow, I will speak to the local clergyman."

THEIR WEDDING MORNING dawned with misty rain filling the skies, but Lucy did not care. She dressed in a lovely blue gown. Anne's maid came in to do her hair, and Annabelle sat on her bed to watch, enthralled by the process. She was in her best rose gown, a crisp bow holding back her curls as she tried not to wrinkle the dress by moving around too much.

The time flew by, and Lucy was ready to go downstairs where Aubrey waited for them. Annabelle took her hand, and they descended the stairs. Richard was waiting at the bottom step, his face solemn.

"Are you ready?" he asked.

"Yes, Uncle Richard," Annabelle answered before Lucy could draw breath.

He smiled and held out his arm. "Then let us go in."

Lucy took his arm and held Annabelle's hand at her other side. Reverend Fuller was waiting in the front parlor, Anne standing to one side and Aubrey next to the cleric. Richard led them to Aubrey, kissed his sister's cheek and stepped back next to his wife. Aubrey stepped forward to stand next to Lucy with Annabelle in the middle, one hand in each of her parents'.

In no time at all Reverend Fuller completed the service and Lucy was married to the one man she had always loved. Aubrey kissed her, trying not to squeeze Annabelle still nestled between them.

"Finally," he murmured.

The minister said his goodbyes and left. He had not been happy about performing the marriage ceremony. He felt it was all quite irregular, but Richard and Aubrey between them had pressed him, and he conceded.

"All the best to you both," Richard said. "We are very pleased for you."

Anne put out a hand to Annabelle. "Perhaps we should go check on Ned and let your Mama and Papa be on their way."

Annabelle gave each parent a kiss, and a curtsy then departed the room with Anne. She was to stay with her aunt and uncle for a few days to give her parents a short honeymoon. Rathburn had been sent off to Hull to board a ship to Brussels, and Lady Lovell had left for her sister's home in London, all the while declaring her innocence in Rathburn's schemes. Lucy thought Aubrey would forgive her in the future just to appease Annabelle, who still wanted to meet her grandmother.

Richard clasped Lucy's hands and kissed her forehead. "I love you, Lucilla. Be as happy with Lovell as I am with my Anne."

Tears threatened again, and Aubrey tucked Lucy against his side. "I think it is time for us to depart. Thank you again for all your aid."

"It is my pleasure. Take good care of my sister."

The carriage was waiting outside ready to take them to Lovell Abbey. Aubrey sat next to Lucy rather than take the backward-facing seat.

"I do not think I have ever been so happy in all my life." Aubrey put his arm around her.

Lucy glanced at him and felt shy. The whole day had felt dreamlike, a fantasy that might not last. But he was warm and solid next to her as she rested her head against his shoulder.

"I love you. I love you so much," she said as her fingers plucked at the sleeve of his jacket.

"Ah, Lucy, I love you too."

The ride was not long, and they pulled up to find the entire staff waiting to meet their new mistress. Lucy knew many of them already but was happy to see how pleased they were at the master's marriage. The servants had not forgotten Aubrey during his years abroad, and they were glad he was back.

After they had gone down the line of servants, Aubrey turned to his housekeeper. "Please send trays up to my room for dinner later." Mrs. Beckham curtsied, and he led Lucy up the stairs to their suite.

She followed him into an elegant sitting room done in blue and gilt. He pointed to a door on the far side of the room. "Your bedroom and dressing room is in there. I apologize that it is not ready for you to use yet. My mother just moved out yesterday. I thought you might want to redecorate it as your tastes might not align with hers."

With a devilish gleam in his eye, he continued, "Or you can just stay with me in my room. I would prefer that, but I know it is not fashionable and you may want your privacy."

Lucy laughed. "I would be perfectly satisfied to move into your room. Do you know where my clothes are stored?"

Aubrey cleared his throat. "I had them unpacked in my room. I had a wardrobe moved in, and there has been space made in the dressing room." He crossed to a door on the other side of the room that was ajar and pushed it open.

Lucy followed him into what was his bedroom. It was furnished in a masculine manner with light green hangings to offset the more massive wood furniture. The room was spacious and had airy, large windows open to let in the sunshine from outside. A maid stood at one wardrobe with Lucy's chests and boxes strewn around her.

"This will do nicely," she said with a smile. The maid looked nervously at Lucy, but Aubrey addressed her first.

"Lady Lucilla, this is Margaret, who will be your temporary maid until or if you make other arrangements. I have told her you are a kind and patient mistress." He smirked at Lucy, and she rolled her eyes back at him. "Margaret, the Viscountess will not need your aid this evening. You can finish unpacking tomorrow and please make it late in the day."

Poor Margaret turned a dark red and bobbed a curtsy, nearly running from the room.

Lucy crossed to Aubrey and put her arms around his neck. "You embarrassed that poor girl."

Aubrey pulled her closer. "I am told that she is competent and pleasant, but if you want to choose differently, please do so. You are the mistress now, and I want you to make any changes you wish at Lovell Abbey."

She tugged at the hair that hung slightly over his collar. "The only change I want right now is for you to undress."

"As soon as I have you unclothed." He pulled her towards the large bed that sat on one side of the bedroom. "Turn around, wife. Let me undo your ties and buttons."

Lucy obediently turned to allow Aubrey access to the top of her dress. Meanwhile, she pulled pins from her hair so that the shining tresses fell down and covered his hands. Aubrey gathered her hair in one hand and pulled it to one side over her shoulder so he could continue to undress her. As the top of the dress sagged he lifted it up, and Lucy raised her arms so he could pull it over her head. Aubrey looked at the curve of her neck and leaned forward to give it a kiss. He trembled with need, so he pulled at the laces of her stays, fumbling at the ties while Lucy leaned back into him and raised an arm to run through his hair. He stopped and ran a hand up her smooth limb, following it with kisses.

Meanwhile, Lucy was pushing at his coat and untying his cravat. "You need to take these clothes off," she murmured.

"I will not last long this first time, love," Aubrey replied. "I have waited too long, but later we will go slowly." Aubrey pulled his shirt off over his head, further disrupting his curls and then attacked his breeches while Lucy pulled off her shoes and stockings. Lucy's eyes were huge as he picked her up and placed her on the bed.

"I have wanted you as my wife and in my bed for so long. You must forgive me if I am overly possessive, but you are mine."

Lucy caressed his cheek, then wrapped a hand around his neck and pulled him down to her.

After they lay together until Aubrey rolled over. He pulled her close, and Lucy put one hand over his heart, feeling the rapid beating slow. He kissed her forehead and pushed curls back, then put his head down with a small smile on his lips.

"What is it?" Lucy asked tenderly.

"I am the luckiest man on earth. I am married to the woman I have dreamed about for years and my daughter I did not even know about last week is coming home to live with us tomorrow."

"You know, she loves Ned. She asked when she would have a baby brother just like him."

Aubrey chuckled. "Well, I am doing my best. If you can give me a few moments, we can try again although she may end up with a baby sister. Would that be as satisfactory to Annabelle?"

"I believe she would grow accustomed to a sister. But I think you have already done your best, sir, and she will have a sibling sooner than she thinks." Lucy turned her face to her pillow, suddenly shy as Aubrey tensed and sat up.

"Are you pregnant? I am to be a father again?" Aubrey shook his head. "I am just getting adjusted to a daughter and now another child."

Lucy sat up with a frown. "Is that a problem? I am not sure yet but the signs...."

Aubrey interrupted, clasping her to him. "Problem? No, it is the best news. This time, I can be with you and see our baby as he grows. Because I think it will be a boy! We dare not gainsay Annabelle."

And so it was the first of three more children who grew and played among the green hills of Yorkshire.

Author's Note

Jerusha Moors grew up in Connecticut but currently lives in Portland, Maine. Her sister introduced her to the books of Georgette Heyer, and she never outgrew her love of romance books, especially from the Regency period. She hopes you enjoy her stories and books about those times and will follow her on social media.

She appreciates you sharing this adventure with her. She will continue to write about Regency romance. Please leave reviews and like her Facebook page: https://www.facebook.com/JerushaMoors/

Books by Jerusha Moors

Available at all major outlets.

Always—Richard and Anne's story (short story)

Abandon—Aubrey and Lucy's story

Advantage—Jamie and Eleanor's story

Admiration — David and Selina's story

Don't miss out!

Visit the website below and you can sign up to receive emails whenever Jerusha Moors publishes a new book. There's no charge and no obligation.

https://books2read.com/r/B-A-LAIH-AHJW

BOOKS 2 READ

Connecting independent readers to independent writers.